SQUALL

NOVELS BY SEAN COSTELLO

Eden's Eyes (1989)

The Cartoonist (1990)

Captain Quad (1991, 2011)

Finders Keepers (2002)

Sandman (2003)

Here After (2008)

SQUALL

A novel by Sean Costello

*Scrivener*Press

Library and Archives Canada Cataloguing in Publication

Costello, Sean, author
    Squall : a novel / Sean Costello.

ISBN 978-1-896350-54-7 (pbk.)

    I. Title.

PS8555.O73S68 2014   C813'.54   C2014-905478-5

Book design: Laurence Steven
Cover design: Chris Evans
Photo of author: Alfred Boyd

Published by Scrivener Press
465 Loach's Road,
Sudbury, Ontario, Canada, P3E 2R2
info@yourscrivenerpress.com
www.scrivenerpress.com

We acknowledge the financial support of the Canada Council for the Arts and the Ontario Arts Council for our publishing activities.

Canada Council Conseil des arts
for the Arts   du Canada

ONTARIO ARTS COUNCIL
CONSEIL DES ARTS DE L'ONTARIO
an Ontario government agency
un organisme du gouvernement de l'Ontario

For Pete Aubé,
my best friend in the world since time out of mind.
Thanks for the laughter, man.

And for my brother, James Martin, fellow survivor.

I love you guys.

1

Friday, January 18, 1:35 a.m.

"Fucking brother of yours," Ronnie Saxon said, the coke revving her up, making her aggressive. "Treats you like his errand boy."

Dale Knight drove the big Dodge Ram without looking at her, knowing the eye contact would only make her worse. He flicked the wipers on, fat snowflakes melting as they struck the windshield. Outside, Asian district neon reflected off the accumulated snow, drifts of it smothering the city.

Ronnie said, "You should be partners by now. Look at him, king shit in that big house in Rosedale. Where are we? Cabbage-town. Half a duplex with a plugged toilet, those fucking rappers upstairs playing that street shit half the night."

She paused to do another hit off her coke mirror and Dale said, "It'll come, Ronnie. Ed's just showing me the ropes. He came up this way himself, doing runs for Copeland. It's how it works."

"The ropes," Ronnie said. "Listen to yourself." She hefted the gym bag out of the foot well in front of her, 250K worth of Randall Copeland's heroin. "I was you? I'd take this shit and start up on my own. Someplace fresh. Miami, maybe."

Dale took the bag from her and tossed it on the back seat. "You're talking shit now, Ronnie. This is Copeland's dope. Randall Copeland? Remember him?"

A long-established independent in the Toronto Area drug trade, Randall 'Randy' Copeland had managed through sheer force of will to maintain a healthy percentage from almost all of the rival factions that had sprung up over the past few decades— the Jamaican posses, the Eastern European *bratvas*, the Asian triads, even the American biker and youth gangs—mostly by providing safe and reliable distribution, his vast clientele far more terrified of Copeland than they were of his competitors.

Dale said, "My brother told me he watched the man split a guy's tongue with a pair of tin shears for lying about putting a ding in his Beemer. He's the last son of a bitch we want to fuck with. Why don't you just mellow out."

Ronnie only stared at him, that hard shine in her eyes that made Dale nervous, giving him no idea what was going on inside her head. It made him realize how little he knew about the girl. He'd met her through his brother—one of Ed's discards, a hand-me-down, like a sweater—and six months later they're engaged. True, she was fine: that black leather coat flared open to show some cleavage above a tight red top, legs that went all the way up, all that thick dark hair. But she never talked about her past, only hinted at its flavour, almost like a threat when she got pissed at him and wanted him to know it: *"There's a lot you don't know about me, Dale, so I suggest you just back off."*

He said, "Listen, we're almost there. I'm gonna go inside and do the deal, you're gonna wait in the truck. Ten minutes tops. We're late, so I'll probably have to put up with some shit about that." Late because Ronnie's 'quick' stop for blow wound up costing them an hour.

"You saying that's my fault?"

"We could have picked up your blow *after* the drop, like I suggested."

"The day I had, you expect me to wait?"

Letting it go, Dale said, "When I come out we're gonna take the money to Ed, collect our two grand and that's the end of it. Fucking coke, makes you hyper."

Ronnie said, "At least I'm awake," but the edge was gone from her tone, something else on her mind now. She slipped the smeared coke mirror into her bag, her trim body moving to the Santana tune on the radio.

Dale slowed the Ram and turned left, then left again into an alley behind a closed Korean take-out joint. He parked beside a black BMW and killed the engine, pocketing the keys. He reached over the seatback for the gym bag and Ronnie leaned into him, her manicured fingers squeezing his thigh.

"I'm sorry I bitched you out," she said, close, minty breath warm in his ear. "I just wanna see us get ahead. We deserve more."

"It'll come," Dale said, suspicious as he always was when she turned on that lovey-dovey shit. But man, she knew how to play him. "Couple more years, maybe we'll move into the top half of the duplex."

"Don't push it, Dale."

Grinning, he got the gym bag and opened the door. "Ten minutes."

"Let me come in with you, baby."

"The mood you're in? I don't think so."

"I'm fine now, honest. Come on, they won't mind."

Dale got out of the truck, sinking to his ankles in wet snow.

"Forget it, Ronnie. These guys are wrapped way too tight. I go in alone."

"But—"

"Lock the doors. It's a bad neighbourhood."

He closed the door on her protest, thinking, *Stick with the plan.* He'd fucked up more than once already, Ed bringing him into his office to ream him out, like Ed was his father instead of his brother. But Dale never took it personally. He *was* a fuck-up a lot of the time, the dope getting him into shit he sometimes couldn't even remember. He'd been clean a few months now, though, even caught a few twelve-step meetings when the itch got bad enough. Truth was, Ed's last talk had shaken him: *"Keep it up, Dale, you're going to find yourself in a bind I can't pry you out of. In this world, blood only runs so thick."* Jesus, Ed could be spooky sometimes.

But he was right. Brothers or not, Ed had put his own ass on the line to get him this job, and if he screwed it up, it was Ed who'd have to answer for it. The job itself was easy—drop off the shit, pick up the cash, bring it to Ed and get paid on the spot. Two weeks' pay at minimum wage in a couple hours. All he had to do was follow the rules.

He banged on the restaurant's steel service door, then glanced back at the Ram—shit, Ronnie smoking in his brother's truck, like he needed more trouble with Ed. He turned to say something to her about it and the service door opened on its chain. An Asian guy the size of an outhouse stuck his face in the gap, shark eyes sizing Dale up, then got the chain off and let him inside.

Dale followed him into a storage area where the boss, Trang, and another guy—all three of these dudes in the same sky blue leisure suits—were shooting darts and drinking beers.

Dale stumbled over something on his way in, making a racket, and Trang missed his shot, looking none-too-pleased about it as he turned to face Dale. "You're late," he said and let his jacket fall open, giving Dale a clear view of the big semi-auto tucked into the front of his trousers.

"Yeah, Mister Trang," Dale said, "I'm sorry. I was ... unavoidably detained. But I got your product right here."

"It makes your brother look bad," Trang said, not letting it go, "showing up late for a quarter million deal." He touched the black leather briefcase that lay on its side on a service table next to him. A caress. "I should tell him."

"Sorry, Mister Trang. It won't happen again."

Trang's gaze ticked over Dale's shoulder now, registering mild surprise. He turned to look at his pals and when he faced Dale again he was smiling, showing small yellow teeth. "But I see you brought us a peace offering," he said, the smile widening. "Blowjobs all around, eh boys?"

The other two joined Trang in a good laugh and Dale turned to see Ronnie right behind him, strolling past him now, cool as ice, going straight to Trang as the other two flanked him to wait their turn.

Dale said, "Ronnie?" but the girl wasn't listening.

She sidled up to Trang with lidded eyes, giving him her smokiest smile, one hand going to his thin chest, the fingers of the other loosening his belt.

Ronnie said, "I'll blow you ... "

And Dale saw her hand close around the pistol grip, saw her shoot Trang in the balls and draw the gun from his pants as he fell, tugging once as it snagged, then watched her drop to one knee to gut-shoot the big one, capping the third in the throat as he reached for his piece. The reports slammed Dale's ears, flat claps of thunder in the cement-walled room. For a moment from the look on her face Dale thought she might turn the gun on him, too.

Then she was moving, sweeping the briefcase off the table, turning to hand it to Dale. He took it and watched her collect the men's wallets and guns, calling Trang an asshole when his bloodied hand came up to clutch her calf, cursing him again for staining her jeans. She stuffed the swag into a plastic bag she found somewhere and it was all Dale could do not to faint dead away.

Then, with the cool detachment of a farm woman snapping the neck of a hen, Ronnie put a single round into the top of Trang's head, stifling his frantic screams. She stood over each of the others in turn, but both were already dead.

"See?" she said, looking at Dale now. "That's how easy it is. Now come on."

She started for the exit but Dale stood frozen, gaping at the scene, gunsmoke smarting his eyes.

Ronnie's voice: "Dale."

"Jesus, Ron…"

"Look at me, Dale."

He did.

"It's like I've told you before," she said, green eyes wildly alive, "there's a lot you don't know about me. Now *come on.*"

Head spinning, Dale broke for the exit, running full out now, briefcase in one hand, gym bag in other.

* * *

Ronnie got right back into the coke, turning the radio up loud, laughing when Dale came out of the alley too hard, fishtailed in the wet snow and sideswiped a parked van.

"*Fuck,*" Dale said and Ronnie whooped. He couldn't look at her, not now, afraid that if he did he'd grab Trang's gun off the console and shoot her with it.

Now she was stuffing the other two guns under her seat,

going through the wallets, griping about cheap chinks who didn't carry cash, tossing things out the window as she got through with them.

Slowing as he turned north onto Yonge Street, Dale said, "You know what you just did?"

"Made us five hundred к in under a minute? Twice that if we cut the shit and deal it ourselves."

"You *killed* us, that's what you did." Picturing Ed when he found out about this, Dale wanted to scream. "Copeland's gonna waste us for this and there's not a thing Ed's gonna be able to do about it."

"Like we're going to sit around and let that happen. The airport's a thirty minute drive from here. If you can't handle it, pull over and I'll take the wheel."

"The airport. In this weather."

Ronnie considered this a moment, staring out at the worsening storm. Then she dialed 411 on Ed's satellite phone, asked for the number for flight information and waited while it connected, shushing Dale when a recorded voice came on and told her all flights had either been canceled or delayed until further notice.

She hung up and said, "Fuck it then, we'll wait it out. How's the Harbor Hilton sound? Room service. Jacuzzi. It's not like we can't afford it."

"Copeland knows everybody in this town, Ronnie. There's no place we can hide. Fucking shitstorm. Look, maybe we should call Ed, tell him Trang went crazy or something, tried to rip us off. Gave us no choice."

"Forget it, Dale. You lie about as well as you fuck."

"Nice."

"You know what I mean. He'd see right through you."

"Look," Dale said, struggling to catch his breath. His heart was triphammering, the image of Trang clutching his bloody crotch making his stomach sick. "I know a place. It's about five hours north of here. My uncle's cottage on Kukagami Lake. It's the last place Ed'd think to look."

Ronnie said, "A cottage," like it was a toilet. "If we're gonna drive, drive *south*, fuck sake. We take turns at the wheel, we're in Miami in two days."

Dale sped the wipers up a notch, the wet flakes heavier now, angling straight in at the windshield. He said, "They got dogs at Customs, Ronnie, can smell dope on your breath. Forget about it. There's no way we're gonna try that. No, if we're gonna run— and I don't see as we got any other choice now—we're gonna have to ditch the dope or sell the fucker before we leave the country. We lay low at the cottage—it's a real nice place on the lake, Ronnie. Heat, electricity, everything. We stay there a day, maybe two, then drive to Montreal. I know a guy there'll take the shit off our hands. Then we head for Europe or maybe New Zealand. Someplace Ed never heard of."

"What if your uncle's at this cottage?"

"He's in Daytona till the end of March, same drill every year. Trust me, the place is abandoned."

Ronnie was quiet after that, the fading adrenaline rush making her sullen. Dale had seen her like this before, brooding silences that went on sometimes for hours and made him nervous, afraid he'd done something to piss her off and he'd wake up in the morning to find her gone.

But right now he liked her this way just fine. He needed time to think.

He got on the 401 and followed it west to the 400, pointing them north now, into the throat of the storm.

2

AT 6:00 O'CLOCK ON THE MORNING of his thirty-first birthday, Tom Stokes dressed quietly in his winter work clothes, then leaned over the bed to kiss his wife Mandy on the forehead.

Mandy opened her eyes to squint up at him in the thin dawn light. She looked annoyed.

Tom said, "Did I wake you? I was trying to keep it down."

"You're a bull," Mandy said and flipped back the covers, showing a very pregnant abdomen. "Come back to bed."

"I'd love to, but I gotta get airborne. Billy Trudeau said he saw a busted window in Outpost Cabin Three." Billy was an Ojibway trapper and guide Tom sometimes hired to look after the hunters and fishermen he rented his outpost cabins to in season. "That means either looters, animals or both. Either way, I want to get it secured so I can be back in time for Steve's party."

Mandy smiled. "My birthday boys. Okay, I'm up."

As she grunted her way into a sitting position, shivering in the morning chill, Tom crept along the hallway to his son's room.

Steve, five years old today, was still sound asleep, tangled in his blankets as he always was, a restless sleeper since birth. Seeing him there, winter pale and so utterly still, Tom felt the same unnerving mix of love and dread he'd felt every morning since they brought the little guy home from the maternity ward: love of a depth he'd never imagined possible... and dread that his son's stillness meant death had crept in to claim him in the night. An irrational fear, maybe—Steve was a healthy, active kid who, apart from those few routine illnesses of early childhood, rarely even caught a cold—but it was a dread that abated only when Tom rested his hand on that tiny chest, as he did now, feeling the rhythmic passage of air that signaled precious life.

He kissed his son on the cheek, then did his best to disentangle him from his blankets without waking him. By the time he got downstairs, Mandy had a pot of coffee brewing and two slices of rye bread in the toaster for him.

As he always did, Tom took his breakfast into the business office on the main floor. He set his toast on the desk but held onto the coffee, sipping it as he checked the weather forecast on the computer, then visually through the big picture window that gave onto Windy Lake where his two planes—a blue and white Cessna 180 and a bright red DHC-2 de Havilland Beaver—stood waiting on their skis, looking stiff and frosty in the gathering light.

The morning was cold but clear, the windsock hanging limp on its pole, no sign of the storm the computer said was raging a few hours south of them now, working its way north. He should be able to get his repairs done and be back in plenty of time to see Steve getting off the school bus.

The family trophy case caught Tom's eye and he idly surveyed its many awards with pride, even though most of them belonged to his wife. Mandy was a crack shot with any kind of firearm. She'd been competing at some of the highest levels since high school, and for a while, before deciding to become a pilot, had been grooming herself for the Olympics. The most exciting events she competed in were the IPSC matches, wicked, action-movie scenarios with gangster popup targets and cardboard mothers clutching babies. It was wild watching her do her thing at these events—and because of them Steve thought he had the coolest mom on the planet. Some of the trophies were pretty impressive, too: poised, gold and silver figures aiming handguns and rifles, the plaques beautifully engraved. He had a couple of things in here somewhere himself... ah, there they were: a three-inch tall gold cup with 'World's Best Dad' inscribed on its base, and a grinning porcelain skull he won at a coin toss at the Azilda Fair. There was a vacant shelf at the top of the unit, reserved for Steve's future accomplishments; and soon enough, those of his still-gestating baby brother as well.

Completing his morning ritual, Tom sat on the love seat in front of the window and finished his breakfast, gazing with pride at the logo on the Cessna 180, the plane he'd be flying this morning: Stokes Aviation.

He wondered what Mandy got him for his birthday.

3

THE WEATHER BROKE ALL OF A SUDDEN, six in the morning, just south of Parry Sound. An hour earlier they'd been sitting at a dead stop behind a tractor-trailer jackknifed across the highway, flares everywhere, an OPP officer coming right up to Dale's window and asking him where they were headed. Dale only stared at the man and Ronnie said, "Kukagami eventually, but we'd be happy to make Parry Sound tonight, find a hotel and get out of this weather." The cop said that was a good idea, flashed Ronnie a smile and went on to the next vehicle. Dale saw Ronnie tuck her handgun—a nickel-plated Colt .380 she carried with her everywhere—back into her bag and thought, *This is a nightmare, somebody wake me up.*

The drive in the snow, slow and hypnotic, had settled Dale's nerves somewhat; but seeing that cop stroll up to the window like that, and then Ronnie, ready to shoot the man in the face, brought it all back hard. He was a fugitive now, running not only from the most ruthless crime boss in the country but from his own brother. The law, too, if the cops got involved. Christ, three dead Asians.

He kept thinking maybe it wasn't too late. He could call Ed, tell him the truth. This wasn't his mess, it was Ronnie's. Maybe—

Ronnie said, "I know what you're thinking."

Trying to get some edge in his tone, Dale said, "You're a mind reader now?"

"You're thinking of calling your brother, am I right? Telling him it was me? You had nothing to do with it?"

"Would I be lying?"

Ronnie said, "*Fuck* those guys, man. This is petty cash to them. Your brother'll get his wrist slapped and life'll go on. Meanwhile we're sipping gin fizzes in the Florida sunshine."

Dale glanced at the phone and Ronnie said, "Okay, you want to call him?" She picked up the receiver and held it out to him. "Be my guest. See what he has to say. Better yet, call Copeland. It's his dope, anyway. And you know how forgiving *he* can be." When Dale didn't move, Ronnie set the phone back in its cradle. "You're in this, Dale. Don't kid yourself. You *are* it. Fucking slant, thinks I'm gonna suck his yellow dick. *What* dick? I hate those slippery creeps, think they can have whatever they want." She said, "Did you see the look on his face?" and brayed laughter.

Dale tuned her out. Let her rant.

Traffic got moving again after that, the drive to Parry Sound slow but smooth.

Then, almost without noticing, Dale was driving on centre-bare blacktop under a white sky, the moon burning through like a dull beacon, guiding them north.

* * *

They stopped for breakfast at an all-night joint along the highway, Ronnie bringing the cash and the drugs inside, bitching about the country music on the radio as she led Dale to a booth by the window. She ordered black coffee, bacon and eggs over hard with white toast and Parisienne home fries and dug in without saying a word.

All Dale could stomach was dry toast and a few sips of apple juice. He'd lost his appetite for food. What he needed now was inside that gym bag. He kept thinking about that first sweet rush when the tourniquet comes off, the warm calm that washes over you like tropical surf, the only true antidote to fear he'd ever found. And he was shit-scared now, more afraid than he'd ever been. Every minute that passed without dealing with this thing was a minute closer to the grave. Until now he'd always been able to turn to his brother when he got in a jam, Ed always coming through for him. But this … this fucking *mess* didn't *have* a solution. At least not one Dale believed he could survive.

He looked at Ronnie looking at him, then down at her plate as she pushed her fork into a small round potato, spun it in a glob of ketchup then tugged it off with her perfect white teeth, eyes full of dark humour.

Dale thought of Trang screaming and felt his stomach clench, the dry toast congealing into a missile shape inside him, and he stood up fast saying, "Goin' out for a smoke," making it through the door just in time to gulp the cold morning air and keep his meager breakfast where it belonged.

He lit a cigarette and leaned against the wall under the overhang, smoking and watching the dark clouds in the south race to catch up with them.

Ronnie came out a few minutes later with her cargo.

"Pay the bitch," she said, "and let's go."

4

WRAPPED IN A HOUSECOAT THAT REFUSED TO CLOSE over her enormous belly, Mandy Stokes sat at the radio console with a headset on, her gaze shifting between the Cessna 180—out near the centre of the lake now, Tom taxiing it into position for takeoff—and the radio controls.

As she ran through some last minute checks with Tom, Steve appeared beside her like a tiny Ninja, giving her a start. Still logy with sleep, he watched through the window as the aircraft accelerated for takeoff, his blue eyes unblinking now, his warm hand tightening around Mandy's wrist.

The plane vanished beyond a long peninsula for a moment, its engine a rising whine in the distance, then reappeared airborne banking north, Tom giving the wings a little side to side tilt, his version of a wave. When Steve saw that, he released his mother's wrist and yawned.

Then Tom's voice came over the radio: "The wildman up yet?"

Mandy said, "You mean up or awake?"

Tom laughed. "Can I talk to him?"

"Mandy said, "You can try," and held the handset out to her son.

Still half asleep, Steve gave her a grumpy look. But he took the handset and said, "Hi, Dad."

"Morning, big guy. Happy Birthday."

"Thanks, Dad. You, too."

"Excited about tonight?"

"Uh huh."

Tom chuckled. "Can't hardly contain yourself, huh, pardner? How old are you now?"

"You know. Five."

"*Five.* About time you got a job then, don't you think? Started earning a living?"

Steve just breathed into the handset.

Tom said, "You gonna be this much fun all day?"

Yawning again, Steve said, "Bye, Dad, I gotta get ready for school."

"Okay, sport. I love you. See you tonight."

Mandy took the handset from her son and signed off with Tom.

Giving her belly a gentle pat, Steve said, "Can I have Frosted Flakes? It's my birthday."

5

RONNIE AND DALE REACHED THE COTTAGE at 7:30, the new day coming on blue and cold as Dale parked the Ram in the yard and got out to find the key. The road in from the highway had been plowed and sanded, only the winding cottage road, a distance of about three miles, requiring 4-wheel drive and a little care.

The cottage itself stood on the last piece of private property on this stretch of side road, perched on the tip of a narrow peninsula where the road dead-ended, the nearest neighbour six miles back, a summer dwelling Dale could see was vacant as they passed it on the way in.

He found the key where Uncle Frank had hidden it since Dale was a kid, in the flared nostril of a grim figure on a thirty foot totem pole Frank had picked up at a yard sale someplace.

He got the front door open and Ronnie pushed past him saying, "I'm going to bed." She snatched the truck keys out of his hand and took the gym bag and briefcase upstairs with her. Dale said, "Make yourself at home," and listened to her—boot heels stabbing the wood floors up there, the squeak of bed springs and then silence—before getting his coat and boots off, turning up the heat and taking a stroll through the place.

Being here, amidst Uncle Frank's weird antler furniture and hunting trophies, made him feel like a kid again. After his mother died and his father buckled down for the serious drinking, Dale had come up here as often as he could. Uncle Frank had always treated him like a prince, teaching him to fish, letting him take the power boat out by himself, and telling him stories about how crime didn't pay and he didn't have to turn out like his brother if he didn't want to. What Uncle Frank never understood was that in those days Dale wanted nothing more. Nobody messed with Ed, that was the thing. Ed always got what he wanted, one way or another, and Ed never felt fear, something Dale had lived with since his mother died, a withered stick figure in a prison hospital bed, eaten alive by cancer while still in her thirties.

Fucking fear.

In the kitchen Dale checked the fridge: a half-used jar of raspberry jam in there, six cans of beer and not much else. He helped himself to one of the beers and sat on the couch facing the big picture window that overlooked the lake. Nothing moving out there in the cold, not even a breeze. The sun was out now, but muted by a white sky that shaded to near black in the south.

The beer tasted flat and Dale set it aside, little comfort there. His demons were awake now, capering and hungry as hell.

He listened into the remote silence of the place, the starkness of it serving only to amplify his need. He glanced at the ceiling, knowing that Ronnie was in the room directly above him, probably already sound asleep. Bitter, he wondered what it said about her feelings for him that she took that bag of dope upstairs with her. The money, too, for that matter. What was he going to do, take off with it and leave her stranded here?

She doesn't want you getting high, the demon said. *Bitch prob-*

*ably filled her own snoot with it before passing out on your uncle's
Posturepedic.*

He said, "Slippery bitch," and headed for the stairwell in his
socks. He knew every creak in the floorboards and risers and
made the trip to the master bedroom without a sound. She'd
pulled the door shut but hadn't latched it, and it opened quietly
on well-oiled hinges. In the dim, Dale saw her lying on her side
with her back to the curtained window, her breathing shallow
and raspy with sleep.

The gym bag was on the foot of the bed next to the briefcase
and Ronnie's jacket and purse. He was almost out the door with
it when Ronnie said, "Put it back," without moving and Dale
said, "Just a taste, Ronnie. That's all. To quiet the voices."

He heard her say, "Asshole," as he pulled the door shut and
set the latch.

Back on the couch, he set the gym bag on his lap and
unzipped it, removing one of the kilo bags of heroin. It occurred
to him as he hefted it that a few good snorts would get him
there, but not like blasting it would—and remembered Uncle
Frank was diabetic.

He found the insulin syringes in a kitchen drawer, thirteen
of them left in a box of fifty, as seductive a sight as anything he'd
seen in their crisp, sterile wrappers. He scooped them up, got
a teaspoon from the cutlery drawer, a wad of cotton from an
aspirin bottle and found a book of matches by the fireplace.

There was a moment of hesitation, a distant voice telling
him not to blow his clean time…then he punched a hole in the
kilo bag with his pocket knife and measured out a hit with the
tip of the blade.

A prickly sweat broke out in his armpits as he cooked
the hit then drew it up through the cotton into the slender

syringe. His mouth was bone dry now and his breath came hot and fast.

He held the syringe up to the light, teasing out the last few bubbles from the amber fluid, warm and amniotic. That same distant voice bade him reconsider, but he was committed now.

The prick of the needle was glassy, inordinately painful, but the feeling passed quickly and he watched with detached fascination as a tiny eruption of blood rose to meet the falling plunger.

6

MANDY SAID, "BETTER GET A MOVE ON, YOUNG MAN, or you'll miss your bus."

Cocooned in his pillowy red snowsuit, Steve came whisking down the hallway, his overstuffed school bag flopping between his shoulder blades. Though he wasn't a big fan of school, the little guy was excited about it today. His JK teacher always made a fuss about the kids' birthdays, and Steve had been chattering about it all morning.

"Miss Sutcliffe always makes a cake," he told her. "I asked for chocolate. And she puts money inside it in wax paper. It's not a surprise. She has to tell us so we don't crack our teeth. Timmy MacNamara got a Toonie last week and it wasn't even his birthday."

Mandy held the front door open for him and Steve barreled past her, stopping on the porch to watch his mom pull on a parka and trade her fuzzy slippers for galoshes. Then he was down the steps and running, skidding to a stop at the verge of the rural road just in time to meet the bus.

Earning a disgruntled "Mu-um!" for her efforts, Mandy lifted him onto that first high step and Steve tramped the rest of the way up, grinning shyly when the driver and some of the other kids shouted, "Happy Birthday, Steeeeeve!"

As the door hissed shut, Mandy felt a bright jab of pain in her side and thought *Oh, shit*; but it passed quickly and she turned to go back inside, watching the big yellow bus chuff its way along the ice-patched road.

She was in the foyer stepping out of her boots when she heard Tom's voice on the radio.

* * *

Tom spoke into the boom mike on his headset, his voice raised against the drone of the aircraft as he taxied toward the outpost cabin on Yorston lake. "This is Quebec-Victor-Bravo on the ice at Outpost Three," he said. "I can see the damage from here."

Mandy's voice in the headset: "Acknowledge, Quebec-Victor-Bravo. Birthday boy. What do you see?"

"Branch through the front window. A bunch of shingles blown off. Gonna be here a while."

"Roger that, QVB. Storm's still headed your way, though, so maybe you should tackle the window first so you can be ready to bolt if the weather starts bearing down on you. You know what you're like once you get started on something."

"Say again, Home Base? There's no one here fits that description."

"You heard me, wise guy. Don't make me come out there. I want you home in one piece *and* on time for Steve's party. Get that right and who knows, maybe we'll have a private party later on."

"Mission understood, but may induce labour."

"Let me worry about that. Home base out."

Smiling, Tom guided the Cessna to a stop twenty feet from

shore and powered down. This past week had been unseasonably cold, even for the Sudbury Basin, temperatures plummeting to a frosty thirty-five below, some days even colder with the wind-chill, and many of the remaining birch trees in the area had been losing their branches, the heftier ones popping off the trunks with sharp pistol cracks. That appeared to be what had happened here, the ejected branch shattering the front window, letting the weather in.

As Tom approached the cabin, bent against a freshening wind, he could see that it wasn't only the weather the shattered glass had allowed inside. A fair-sized animal, a lynx, maybe, or a restless raccoon, had gotten in there, too. *God damn.* Supplies torn up. Curls of frozen animal shit all over the place.

Oh, well, Tom thought. *Cost of doing business.*

He set about wrestling the heavy branch out of the window frame, deciding to cut down the parent tree in the spring and chainsaw it into stove lengths.

As the branch pulled free and Tom dragged it clear, trying not to topple himself in the knee deep snow, he saw the amber eyes of a lynx, almost certainly the culprit, tracking him from the edge of the bush. He said, "I don't suppose you're going to help," and the skittish animal turned tail and bolted into the woods.

Tom thought, *Beautiful.*

After a quick scan of the sauna shed, still intact, he unlocked the cabin door and let himself inside. He thought of getting a fire going in the wood stove, but with that frosty wind picking up now, setting off a low howl as it gusted through the open window frame, he could see little point in wasting the wood. He got the plastic garbage bin from the kitchen and started picking up the glass.

As he worked Tom realized that in spite of the occasional

nuisance like this, his life was exactly as he'd always imagined it. He'd married his college sweetheart, fathered a beautiful boy—with another one ready to pop out and say howdy any day now; Mandy had refused the ultrasonographer's offer to tell her the baby's sex, but Tom had wanted to know—and the once flagging business that was originally his dad's had finally started to thrive. Tom had always loved the outdoors, so his transition into the family business had seemed a natural one. They owned a half dozen cabins on some of the most remote and well-stocked lakes in the North, hauled cargo to otherwise inaccessible mining sites, and ran a small, year-round flight school, which Mandy managed when she wasn't busy being pregnant. Life was good.

There were some scraps of plywood under the stilted cabin, left over from building the sauna shed, and Tom reckoned he could use those to board up the window until he could get a new piece of glass cut. He'd have to shovel a bit of snow to get at them, but that wouldn't take too long.

He got a shovel out of the storage bin on the deck and paused to study the sky in the direction of home: stormy all right, low and threatening, but still a long ways off. If he played his cards right, he could get the window boarded up, scrape the lynx shit off the floor, tack those shingles back on and maybe even fell that birch tree and cut it into stove lengths.

Shivering in the wind, Tom set himself to the tasks at hand.

7

DALE CAME AWAKE WITH A KINK IN HIS NECK, sitting on the couch with his head slung back, a strand of drool connecting his chin to a wet spot the size of a saucer on his Tragically Hip T-shirt. The sky outside the picture window was dense with cloud cover now, and a light snow was falling. There was no sign of Ronnie.

He glanced at his watch, mildly surprised to see that it was past four in the afternoon. He gave his head a shake and leaned over his works, spread out on the raw-pine coffee table in front of him. A quick inventory told him he'd already used three of the syringes, though he could only remember the first. The reason he was here rose up in the fog of his mind and Dale decided it was time for a little pick-me-up.

He got it done quickly, nodded off briefly, then got up to go to the john. That done, he felt around in his coat pockets for his cigarettes before remembering he'd left them in the truck. He got his boots and coat on and went outside.

Halfway across the yard he heard Ed's phone ringing in the Ram. He thought, *Fuck,* and tramped through the snow to answer it, Ed's voice coming at him before he got the handset to his ear.

"Dale? Answer me, dipshit. Is that you?"

"Yeah, Ed, it's me."

"It was the coke whore, am I right? Your fian*cée*? Tell me I'm right, Dale."

He considered lying—for all the good it would do him—then thought, *Screw it, I told her to wait in the truck.*

He said, "Yeah, Ed. It was Ronnie."

"I fucking *knew* it. You know what I've got to do now, Dale? I've got to go see Randall Copeland and explain this to him. Tell him how my dipshit brother and his coke whore slaughtered three of his best customers. How you then stole his product *and* his money and tried to make a run for it. Jesus Christ, Dale, how many times do I have to tell you? When you do a job for me, you repre*sent* me. How many times?"

There was a pause, Ed waiting for an answer, but Dale couldn't think of what to say, the dope making him want to giggle.

Ed said, "Are you high?"

"Maybe a little."

Ed gave a dry chuckle. "You're a piece of work, bro, I'll give you that. A real piece of work. All right, listen. This still might be fixable. You get the cash and the product back to me a-sap, all I've got to do then is convince Copeland he doubled his money. Where are you right now?"

Dale said, "We're—" and felt the phone snatched out of his hand. He turned to see Ronnie in her jeans and red tank top pitching the phone as far as she could into the woods. When she faced him again she had the .380 in her hand, the stubby muzzle aimed at his face.

She said, "I ought to shoot you myself, save Copeland the trouble."

The sight of that muzzle, the tension in Ronnie's trigger

finger, Ronnie barely dressed out here in the snow, cut through Dale's buzz like a scalpel blade.

He said, "Ronnie, wait. Ed was pissed, sure, but he sounded okay about it, like he could smooth things over with Copeland."

"Did you tell him where we are?"

"No."

"Dale?"

"*No.* You took the phone before I could."

She glanced at the Ram. "What about the truck? Doesn't it have one of those GPS tracking dealies in it? So they can find it if it's stolen?"

Dale shook his head. "It did when Ed bought it, but he had it removed, in case he needed to flee in it someday. Besides, who'd be stupid enough to steal Ed's truck?"

Ronnie just stared at him, vapour jetting from her flared nostrils. Then she lowered the gun, turning into the wind to go back inside. "I can't sit around here much longer," she said, not looking at him. "We leave together—tonight—or I leave alone and to hell with you."

Breathing hard, Dale followed her inside.

8

ED BARKED HIS BROTHER'S NAME into the handset a couple more times—"Dale? *Dale!*"—but it was clear the dummy was gone.

He cradled the receiver and looked across his desk at the two men Randall Copeland had given him as enforcers, Sanj and Sumit Sengupta, thirty-something East Indian brothers with meticulously coiffed hair and a peculiar skill set that made them ideally suited for the job. And although they always did exactly as they were told, without hesitation or complaint, Ed had never quite gotten used to them. Two Bollywood-handsome dudes in expensive suits and Armani overcoats who had no qualms about torturing a man for hours after they'd gotten what they wanted out of him, and then carving him up into tidy Glad Bag-sized fillets for disposal. And while from a businessman's perspective Ed understood the necessity of the process, the fact that these guys clearly relished doing it gave him the willies, pure and simple.

Of the two, though, Sumit, the youngest, creeped Ed out the most. He was the instigator, the one who always took things too far. The man had a genuine taste for the wet work. Ed suspected that Copeland gave his lieutenants crazy fuckers like these to remind them of what lay in store should they ever decide to step out of line. And it was working like a charm today.

Ed got up and stood behind the brothers, knowing it made them nervous. He said, "I know where he is."

One of Trang's men had called him in a panic about an hour ago, describing in broken, rapid-fire English the bloody mess at the take-out joint. Fortunately for the caller, he'd been out doing another buy during the exchange and had come back hours later to find the three men dead, Trang with his balls blown off. And now Ed had to deal with it.

Dale had left him no choice.

He said, "One night when we were kids he decided to take the old man's Caddy out for a joyride, but the dipshit ran over the old man's dog backing out of the garage. Dale panicked and decided to run away. Drove all the way to our uncle's cottage on Kukagami Lake. Dimes to donuts, that's where he is."

Turning in his chair, Sanj said, "So what now?"

"Now I gotta go see Copeland."

Sumit stood. "I'll get the car."

Ed said, "No, I'll do it. You two take Sumit's Mercedes, it's got four-wheel drive." He took a key out of his vest pocket and handed it to Sanj saying, "Spare key to the Ram; try to bring it back in one piece." Then he returned to his desk and started drawing a map. "It's a long drive, but easy enough to find."

When he was done, he handed the map to Sanj and said, "He's an asshole, no escaping that. So far over the line right now Jesus Christ Himself couldn't save the kid. But he's still my brother." He got a cylinder snub-nose .45 out of a desk drawer, kissed the tip of a single round before chambering it, then handed the gun to Sanj. "Quick and painless, understood?"

Sanj said, "Yeah, Ed. It's my specialty."

9

Adjusting his boom mike, Tom said, "This is QVB airborne over Yorston Lake, ETA Home Base in approximately one hour."

Mandy's voice in his headset: "Acknowledge, Quebec-Victor-Bravo. That storm front reach you yet?"

Leveling off at two thousand feet, Tom said, "Still creeping this way, but I think I can get around it. What's it like there?"

"Flurries right now, but it's pretty dark out your way. Birthday or not, Tom Stokes, you put down and wait it out if you have to. Steve'll understand."

Tom said he would, but he hated the idea of missing his son's birthday; and what made it even more special was the fact that they shared a birth date. How often did that happen? Tom saw it as the most important occasion of his life now. And he was already running late, dusk less than an hour away. He'd hoped to meet his son as he got off the school bus.

Mandy had been right, of course. If there was work to be done, he couldn't resist doing it. Just like his dad. He could have split those stove lengths another day and been home with plenty of time to spare. And that sky was looking much worse now than he was letting on.

Mandy said, "I know what you're thinking."

Tom reduced power to seventy-five percent, settling in at a cruising speed of 125 knots. He said, "Oh? And what might that be?"

"Promise me you'll sit it out if the weather gets bad."

"Roger that. Any rug rats show up yet?"

"Nice try, Stokes. I need you to *promise* me you'll sit it out if it gets bad out there."

"Trust me."

Mandy said, "That's how I got pregnant the first time," and Tom laughed.

He said, "Mandy, I promise, okay?"

"You'd better."

"How *is* the bump?"

"I think of it more as a Buick," she said, and Tom pictured her wedged into the rolling chair in front of the desk at home, leaning over the huge mass of her belly to reach the Comlink handset. She was already three days overdue.

He said, "Wouldn't it be wild if you delivered today?"

Chuckling, Mandy said, "I don't even wanna think about it." She said, "Steve just got off the bus," and Tom could almost see the little guy hopping down off that high step with only his face showing in his red snowsuit, waving to his mom in the window. "Wanna say hi?"

"You know I do."

While he waited Tom reduced power again and began a gradual descent, a squall coming up on him all of a sudden. The sky ahead was sheer gunmetal now, forward visibility less than a mile, and it occurred to Tom that he might actually have to take his wife's advice and sit this one out.

He glanced out the side window at the terrain below: blunt

stone hills dotted with scrub; lakes of all sizes, flat, blue-white patches amidst the humps of pre-Cambrian rock. In a few minutes he'd be over the Kukagami tourist area; if he did have to put down, chances were good he could find a cozy ice-fishing shack and some company to pass the time with.

At a thousand feet he banked left, thinking if he got lucky he could flank the worst of it, lose only twenty minutes or so.

Then that sweet little voice was in his head, subdued as it always was when his son talked to him over the radio.

* * *

Red-faced from the cold, Steve took the handset from his mom and said, "Hi, Dad."

"Hey, big guy," Tom said, his voice scratchy with static now. "Happy Birthday."

"Happy Birthday, Dad. Will you be home soon?"

Tom said, "Before you know it," and the doorbell rang.

Steve said, "Someone's here," and took off running, almost dropping the handset passing it back to his mom.

"I bet that's Fran and her daughter April," Mandy said into the mike. "I think our boy's a little sweet on her."

Tom replied, but his words were garbled by static now. With fresh concern Mandy said, "Tom, are you reading me?" and Steve came bombing into the room with April, a tiny five year old cutie in a frilly pink party dress. Fran, the girl's mom, came in as Steve pressed his ear to his mother's belly and invited April to do the same.

Ignoring them, Mandy said, "Tom? *Tom!*" and everyone took a tentative step back, forming a silent tableau around her.

* * *

Tom heard his son say, "Someone's here," through a burst of static, then lost contact. There was some turbulence now, a couple of solid bumps, then a real good one, the Cessna dropping like a stone for about thirty feet, giving Tom that weightless feeling in his gut.

He heard his wife's voice in fragments now—"...sky...dark out there...set down..."—then nothing but static. White noise.

He banked the aircraft away from a towering storm cloud and started looking for a place to land.

10

EVEN THROUGH HER ANGER RONNIE NOTICED the sound—the distant buzz of a small aircraft—and thought it odd, someone out flying on a day like this. But the thought was gone as quick as it came and she bent over her coke mirror for the last two lines, cool crystals bracing her nerves through a cocktail straw.

Fucking Dale. Like talking to a wall.

It boggled her mind how she wound up with wimps like him. It was her only weakness, falling for puppy dogs like Dale, little boys who needed their mommies. When she thought about it, which was as little as possible, she guessed it was because stronger men always ended up treating her like property. Dale, at least, showed her respect. Still, she wished he'd grow a pair right now. She'd told him a half hour ago to get his shit together, they were leaving, and what does he do? Another hit of smack, then runs himself a bath. Fucking moron.

"You're a waste of skin," Ronnie said, straightening now, her husky voice raised. "You hear me, Dale?"

She looked down the hall at the closed bathroom door, then out through the picture window at the storm that had come up all of a sudden, hard flakes riding in off the lake on a bitter wind.

Unbelievable. What in the name of Christ was she doing in a shit hole like this?

"I'm getting out of this deep freeze," she said, shouting now. "You want to sit here and wait for a bullet, be my guest, but I am gone."

She went back to gathering her things—coke mirror, cigarettes, pink Bic lighter, the Colt .380—stuffing it all into her leather bag. It was pointless talking to Dale when he was wasted, but she wanted to sting him, stick it in and break it off. If they'd headed south like she said, not looked back until they hit Miami…

"Ziggy said I could come crib with him," Ronnie said, aiming her words at the bathroom door. "Anytime. Can you picture it, Dale? Ziggy's condo in Palm Beach? Unlimited coke? Ziggy's big black dick—and me. Are you getting all *that* in Panavision, you junkie fuckweed?"

She paused, listening, then picked up the gym bag and the briefcase, liking it's heft. She strode down the hall to the front entrance, side-kicking the bathroom door on her way by.

"Asshole."

In the foyer she set her cargo on the mat and pulled on her coat, not bothering to do it up. She said, "Last chance, Dale. You coming or not?" When she got no reply, she walked back to the bathroom door and shoved it open. She stood in the doorway, looking at the back of Dale's head, all that was visible over the rim of the old clawfoot tub. There was a collapsible dinner tray Dale had set up next to the tub with his smokes and lighter on it, his works and a couple of beers from his uncle's fridge. Trang's 9mm Beretta was on there, too.

"You're going to die, Dale," Ronnie said. "If Copeland doesn't do you for ripping him off, you're going to O.D. Either way, you can count me out."

She tugged Dale's engagement ring off her finger and tossed it into the tub. It landed with a soft *plip* between his splayed legs and sank in lazy arcs to the bottom.

"Till death do us part," Ronnie said. "Look at you, man. You're already dead."

She watched him a moment longer, still as a statue in the tub, too stoned to see what was happening. Then she picked up the dope and the money and went out the front door into the storm, in her anger barely aware of the small aircraft, closer now, and it's faltering engine.

The truck started on the first try and Ronnie drove out of the yard without looking back.

11

"This is Home Base calling Quebec Victor Bravo," Mandy said, fighting a wave of nausea. She'd had terrible morning sickness with this pregnancy, the kind that lasted all day, and stress only made it worse. "Come in, please. QVB, are you reading me? Tom?"

Earlier, after doing her best to assure Steve that everything was going to be fine, she'd asked Fran to take the kids out to the family room and get them started on a video game or something. As if on cue, the doorbell rang again and Steve got right back into the birthday spirit, racing out to see who it was. That had been ten minutes ago, minutes that dragged like hours, and now her throat was parched with the strain of her repeated, fruitless calls over the radio.

Fran came into the room now, saying, "Any luck?"

Mandy put on her game face and shook her head.

"I'm sure he's fine," Fran said, patting Mandy's shoulder. "And don't worry, I'll stay as long as you need me."

"Thanks, Fran. I'm going to give him another five minutes, then I'm going to call Search and Rescue in Trenton and put them on alert."

Mandy returned to the radio then, resuming her efforts to reach her husband. Fran lingered a moment, then returned to the family room, the place alive now with chattering kids, squalling kazoos and the manic rev of video game engines.

12

Ed Knight arrived at Randall Copeland's Hamilton mansion as the sun was going down. Copeland kept an armed guard at the wrought-iron gate and Ed gave the poor jackass a sympathetic wave. Twenty-five below and the mook was standing out here in a fall jacket and driving gloves, his pocked face the colour of brick.

"Use the side entrance," the mook said, teeth chattering, and Ed drove past him shaking his head.

Another hard-on met him at the side door, this one in a strappy T-shirt showing slabs of muscle, and stared at him while he stepped out of his overshoes. The guy frisked him thoroughly, then led him downstairs to a thirty-seat home theater where Copeland sat alone, sipping a cocktail and watching a Jackie Chan movie.

He saw Ed come in and waved him over, muting the volume as Ed took a seat next to him. Copeland was a big man in his late fifties with the imposing thickness of one who still possessed great physical strength but, through a life of continual excess, had managed to insulate himself in a layer of fat that seemed dense enough to deflect bullets. In Copeland's case, this was almost literally true. A couple of years back, in the can at one of his favourite restaurants, a rival crime boss had pumped three .38 calibre rounds into his belly and Copeland had still managed to break the man's neck before walking back to the bar to call an ambulance.

"Ed," Copeland said now, his tone, like his expression, unreadable. "Thanks for coming in on such short notice. It's about your brother."

Ed said, "Yeah, Mister Copeland, I know."

Copeland leaned closer, touching Ed's knee, the rings on his beefy fingers worth more than Ed's house.

"I hate to have to say this to you, Ed. If anybody understands about family, it's me. But Ed, he fucked me, and I can't let that slide. Number one, it's bad for business. And number two, it hurts." Copeland sighed, a sound of immeasurable weariness. "I got a tattoo on my ass, know what it says?"

"No."

"Exit only."

Copeland looked up at the screen now, turning the volume back on, saying, "This is my favourite bit." On the screen Jackie Chan laid out a couple of bad guys with the splintered halves of a pool cue. "What an athlete."

Ed tensed as Copeland muted the volume again and shifted his dull gaze back to him. The way it was going, Ed figured he had about a fifty-fifty chance of walking out of here alive.

Copeland said, "Now here's the situation the way I see it. That little cocksucker's got my money *and* he's got my smack. I'm giving you twenty-four hours to drop them both right back here in my lap. That'll get your brother's dick partway out of my ass."

"I understand, Mister Copeland."

"The rest, handle it any way you like. Neat. Humane. I don't give a shit. Because if I've got to do it, it's going to be slow, it's going to be messy, and I'm going to handle it personally."

"I'm glad you see it that way," Ed said, relaxing a little, "because Sanj and Sumit are on their way to him right now."

"Really?" Copeland said, grimly amused. "You bastard. Those two Punjabs give *me* the creeps."

"I apologize for acting on my own here, Mister Copeland, but like you said, it's family."

Copeland smiled. "Ed, as always, it's a pleasure doing business with you. You anticipate my every need. I can't believe you came out of the same nutsack as that piece of shit brother of yours."

Then the smile was gone, the volume was back on and Copeland had returned his attention to the film.

On his way out, Ed glanced back startled as Copeland barked laughter at something on the screen. Muscle-shirt met him at the door and followed him to the exit to retrieve his overshoes. Ed didn't breathe again until he was in his car.

13

THE STORM FRONT ROLLED OVER the labouring Cessna like an avalanche, sheering winds broadsiding the small aircraft, forward visibility dropping to almost zero in the whiteout. Tom angled that last gut wrenching drop into a steep descent, leveling out at five hundred feet, trying to maintain visual contact with the ground. Under normal circumstances his best option would have been to double back, put down at the cabin and wait it out there. But the engine was running rough now, almost stalling as he fought to stabilize the lightweight four-seater. It was time to land.

In his headset, through the unwavering rasp of static, he could hear his wife's voice—high, fragmented, concerned—and though certain she couldn't hear him, he spoke to her in calming tones, telling her everything was fine, she was right, he'd put down on a lake and sit this sucker out.

He descended to three hundred feet and banked into a tight turn, deciding the lake he'd just flown over was his best bet. Leveling out, he came in low over the treetops, into the wind, watching for the shoreline through the frosted side window. A gust hammered him as he spotted the demarcation between rock and lake and the Cessna dropped sharply, the crown of a giant pine bumping the fuselage beneath his feet.

Then he was out over a formless plain of white with no visible horizon, barely able to see the whirring prop in front of him. The rocky shore was to his right and he angled toward it, squinting out the side window, trying to keep about three wing spans between himself and the ghostly blur of rock and trees. He was coming in too fast but he was committed now.

The skis touched down hard, snow coming up in twin rooster tails, jarring things loose in the cockpit. Tom throttled back, his ground speed dangerously fast, and the Cessna struck a drift, going airborne again. The plane tilted shoreward as gravity reclaimed it, the starboard ski slamming down first. Then the port ski pounded the ice and Tom's left temple struck the door frame, the impact dazing him. Through watery eyes he saw the shoreline sweep around in front of him as a narrow peninsula materialized in the windscreen. There was no time to do anything but kill the engine.

The glare ice propelled him to a patch of shoreline cleared of rock, a beachfront, Tom realized, and now he was plowing up the smooth embankment toward a building looming into view, a cottage with a huge picture window, a neat black hole dead ahead in the amorphous swirl of the storm.

He looked at the photo of his wife and son clipped to the visor as the prop shredded the plate glass and the stout window frame sheered off the wings and skis, reducing the aircraft to a screeching torpedo.

He thought of his unborn child and something came through the windscreen and struck him a glancing blow on the forehead, and for a few blessed moments the shattered world around him went dark.

14

THE SLAM OF THE FRONT DOOR STARTLED DALE, Ronnie's rant
up to that point little more than a distant irritation, a ticking
mechanical clock in a room in which sleep seems so inviting.
He opened his eyes to red slits, the abrupt noise killing his buzz.

Bitch, he thought, and glanced down at the engagement
diamond sending dull sparkles into the deep pool of bathwater that was just beginning to chill. He wanted to feel righ-
teous about it, but all he felt was afraid. How was he going to
get out of this? Short of suicide, he could imagine no other
way. And until that thought—a grim alternative, but at least
one he could control—broke bright and fully formed in his
awakening consciousness, the despair he felt was nigh on
overwhelming.

He glanced at the gun on the tray next to the tub and thought,
Too nasty. No way he could put that sucker in his mouth and
squeeze the trigger. Must be like being hit by a semi. It would be
the way Copeland's guys would do him. Or his brother's. And
it occurred to him then that it would probably go down that
way, Copeland telling Ed to do it himself or Copeland would
handle it personally. Dale had heard some of the stories—the

heinous shit Copeland would do to a guy who'd pissed him off before letting him die—and knew that Ed would feel obliged to arrange it himself.

Jesus, his own brother. That was how far over the line he'd crossed.

And that meant those two goons Ed kept around like trained apes would probably already be hunting him. Those guys were eerie, the way they could find a man no matter how deep he buried himself.

He had to think. There was no way out of this frozen hell-hole now. Fucking Ronnie, could've waited a couple more hours, given him time to sort things out. All he could hope for now was that Ed would expect him to run, send those two psychos on a wild goose chase...

The heroin was trying to reclaim him and as tempted as he was to let it, Dale fought it now, giving his head a violent shake. The action created a moment of clarity and Dale listened into a silence marred only by the steady drip of the faucet... and something else. He thought, *Is that a plane?* and the thought was gone, his mind flipping back to the problem at hand.

He picked up the gun in one wet hand, surprised by its heft, then set it down again. His gaze fell next on the heroin he'd skimmed from Copeland's stash. That'd be the way to do it. He'd O.D.'d a few times already.

Like going to sleep...

The problem was, he didn't want to die. He was twenty-eight years old with a grade nine education, a secret dream of opening his own pizza joint and a love for his brother as big as a boxcar. And now his brother was going to kill him—had no choice, really—because Dale thought with his dick instead of his brain. "That broad is trouble," Ed had told him when Dale first hooked up with her. "She'll take you places you don't want to go." He should've listened.

It was getting hard to think. The water was cold now, his lean body starting to shiver. Another hit, that was the ticket. Just a small one. Get back to level, then sort this shit out.

And there it was on the tray, waiting for him in its syringe like a patient lover. He couldn't even remember cooking it up.

He picked up the syringe with a hand that was steady now, and as he injected the drug in a warm bolus and the shivering stopped, he thought that fucking plane must be flying awfully low—

Then the wall to his right exploded and the prop of Tom Stokes' Cessna struck the side of the tub with its dying revolutions, snapping off in a hail of sparks, the leading edge of the fuselage missing Dale's head by bare inches as he slid under water in a reflex action of lightning speed. Above him the belly of the plane scraped across the rims of the tub with a hellish screech, the sound amplified in Dale's ears by the watery casket he now found himself in. There was a tremendous pain in his left forearm, a spike of shattered 2x4 skewering it, and a precious gulp of air boiled out of his gaping mouth.

Then everything was still and Dale was drowning in his uncle's bathtub.

* * *

Within seconds of the blow to his head Tom jerked into full consciousness, certain he was still in motion and the killing impact was about to come…but the plane was stationary now, and, incredibly, he was still alive.

He did a quick inventory, moving his arms and legs, probing his chest and abdomen for obvious wounds. There was blood in his eyes from a gash at his hairline, the cut small, maybe a half-inch long, and he could taste blood, his bottom lip split and tender to the touch. Otherwise he believed he was fine, though he knew he could still be at risk from internal injuries or shock.

Gingerly, he attempted to extract himself from the cockpit, slipping his seatbelt off and shifting his weight toward the buckled door…but he was trapped, debris across his thighs pinning him, the effort making his head spin. He gave the sensation a few seconds to pass, then pressed his shoulder to the door, trying to force it open. No luck there, the mechanism jammed.

He shifted again, squinting out the shattered side window through swirls of dust and snow, trying to see where he'd wound up—and felt something bump the floor beneath his feet, two quick thumps, blunt and deliberate.

Then he thought he heard a scream, except it sounded like it was coming from under water.

* * *

Dale opened his eyes to see the white underbelly of a small aircraft—he could actually read the word *Cessna*, black letters wavering in the slosh of bathwater, bare inches from his face— the buckled metal breaking the surface, making it impossible for him to raise his head and take a breath. Angling his head back, he could see an oblong of light above and behind him, revealing a space big enough to poke his head through—his syringe was up there, bobbing mockingly with the business end aimed straight down at him—but when he tried to push himself upward he realized that whatever had skewered his arm had him pinned like a bug on Bristol board and he needed to *breathe*. He tried to free his arm with his other hand, but the fucker was locked in tight and now he punched the bottom of the plane, two quick shots. And when he understood that he was drowning, actually *drowning* in his uncle's bathtub, he screamed and lost half of his precious air.

He tried pushing next, heaving one handed against the obstruction above him, a pointless effort that cost him a fresh parcel of air, a surge of bubbles that rose wasted to the surface, flattening against the immovable fuselage before skittering off in all directions.

Dale thought, *The plug!*, and reached for it with his free hand, scrunching down as far as the narrow tub would allow, and the tips of his fingers just...touched it, brushing its cracked rubber edge, but he couldn't *get* it, couldn't reach that vital centre ring, and his chest was on *fire* now, the urge to suck air more powerful than any he'd ever experienced. *Fuck.* There wasn't even a raised lip he could coax out, the fucking plug was firmly seated, and when he tried to lever it up by pressing down on the nearest edge it served only to seat the thing deeper.

Something detonated in Dale's brain, a galvanizing electrical impulse, bursting glare-white and blinding against his retinas.

His throat clicked open and water leaked in, a cold streamer that triggered a violent coughing fit, the last depleted ounces of gas in his lungs pistoning up to expel the liquid—but another cold rush replaced it and Dale slammed his mouth shut, his eyes bugging out of his head now from the pressure inside him, and he thought of his toes, his fucking *toes*, and he curled them around that tiny metal ring with the dexterity of a chimp and the plug let go, the water beginning to drain, he could *feel* the pressure of it against his skin, but it was *too fucking late* and Dale levered his head upward, pressed his pursed lips to the shell of the plane and prayed...

Then the water peeled away and there was a millimetre of

air, blessed *air*, and Dale sucked it in, a thin slip at first, then great whooping lungfuls as the water level fell, and he coughed and spluttered and the tub drained around him, leaving him shivering and impossibly weak.

When he caught his breath Dale said, "Holy fuck," and thought he heard a muffled voice—"Is somebody there?"—but he closed his eyes and breathed, still relishing the sheer glory of drawing air.

The voice came again and Dale felt the winter wind twisting in to find him now, spitting icy flakes that stung his skin. He gave his head a shake, the reality of the situation dawning fully on him only now: a fucking *plane* had just crashed through the wall and landed right on top of him, this deep old clawfoot tub the only reason he was still alive, and now there was somebody out there. Dale thought it must be someone who'd seen the crash, a guy on a snow machine maybe, because there was no fucking *way* it was the pilot. Who could survive a crash like this?

Raising his voice against the howl of the wind, Dale said, "Hang on," and turned his attention to the wooden stake in his forearm. It was attached at its base to a broken stud that still had a chunk of bathroom wall attached to it, the stud trapped between the edge of the tub and the wreckage of the plane. A thick sliver had splintered partway off and speared his arm, driving it against the inside wall of the tub, blood dripping listlessly from it now to stain the remaining water pink. The sucker was in there pretty good and it wasn't until Dale got his knee against it that he was able to rip the spike away from the stud. It looked like it should hurt like hell, but his last hit of smack had taken care of that.

With his injured arm free now, Dale slithered first his good arm, then his head and shoulder up through that oblong of space, all he could fit through the jagged hole. He had to squint through gusts of snow and plaster dust, but it was a hell of a scene, the aircraft itself resting maybe a foot in front of him, having slammed through the picture window out there, then through the bathroom wall before coming to rest with its nose crumpled against the tiled wall to his left. The fuselage was mostly intact, but canted away from him so that Dale could just see the bottom edge of the window in the pilot's door.

Incredibly, the collapsible dinner tray with Daytona Beach, Florida painted on it was still standing next to the tub, its contents undisturbed.

Dale said, "Holy fuck," and that voice came again, a man's voice, clearer now: "Is somebody there?" and Dale said, "Yeah," feeling a dull wonder when he realized the voice was coming from inside the plane. He said, "You're alive, I can't believe it," and the guy said, "That makes two of us," and told Dale his name.

Dale said, "Pleased to meet you, Mister Stokes," and blacked out for a while.

15

MANDY SAT AT HER DESK with the office phone pressed to her ear, shifting impatiently, wincing at the occasional cramp in her belly. Steve had crept in a few moments earlier and stood mutely behind her now, his pointy birthday hat in his hand, the party still going strong in the other room.

After failing to reestablish contact with Tom, Mandy had called Search and Rescue in Trenton. She'd started to explain the situation to the guy who answered, but the bozo said, "One moment, please," like she was ordering take-out, and put her on hold. That's where she was now, listening to the drone of an FM station, the minutes since she'd last heard Tom's voice adding up with excruciating insistence.

Now Steve said, "Mom," in his tiniest voice and Mandy almost jumped out of her skin. Her reaction startled him and he cried out, and Mandy shifted in her chair to face him, seeing tears standing in the poor kid's eyes. Doing her best to smile, she told him she was sorry, he was her little Ninja and she hadn't realized he was there.

Steve tried to return his mother's thin smile, but the tears got away on him and he crawled up onto her lap, his weight against her pregnant abdomen producing a deep spike of pain. Mandy thought, *Please God, not now*, and adjusted the boy's position, shifting him off her belly... and felt his tears spill warm on her arm. She said, "Shh, baby, shh," and stroked his silky hair. "Your daddy's going to be fine."

Fran came into the room now, the party noise swelling behind her as the door swung all the way open. "Steve?" she said. "It's piñata time. Birthday boy gets first swing."

Hiding his face, Steve clutched his mother's arm and Mandy said, "He's okay here with me, Fran. Thanks."

Fran said, "Any news?" and Mandy's face turned beet red, fear and fury finally breaking loose in her. "God damn Search and Rescue's got me on hold," she said, almost shouting the words. "Can you believe it? My husband's missing and they've got me listening to Gino fucking *Vanelli*."

Steve started sobbing quietly.

Barely aware of Fran and her son now, Mandy said, "Come on, come *on*," into the phone, her free hand clutching the bulge of her abdomen as if to keep it from bursting.

16

DALE HEARD THE GUY IN THE PLANE SAY, "Are you still there?" but didn't reply, his foggy mind needing a few more seconds to register again what had happened here. As it dawned on him he said, "Holy *fuck*," and realized he was freezing, the tub completely drained now, winter air finding him through every nook and cranny in the mound of wreckage that surrounded him.

The guy, Tom Stokes, said, "Listen, man, can you give me a hand up here? I'm stuck."

Dale said, "*You're* stuck. Have a look at me."

"Angle's bad, can't see…"

"Then let me paint you a picture. I'm sitting in the bathtub down here, and you're fucking *air*plane is parked right in my lap."

Dale heard the guy giggle, then heard him say," We're in the bathtub together?" and Dale said, "You think it's funny?" Tom Stokes said, "I don't even know your name," and his giggle escalated into deranged laughter.

Dale said, "Asshole."

Then both men were laughing like lunatics, both of them caught in this giddy expression of relief, of death narrowly avoided.

When it settled enough that he could speak, Dale said,

"The name's Dale, and when I said you were in the tub with me I wasn't kidding. I was taking a bath when you came through the wall. I'm butt naked down here, frozen cock stiff, I nearly drowned and I'm completely trapped by all this horseshit. Jesus *Christ* it's cold."

Tom said, "Where are you exactly?"

Dale said, "Right below you," and banged his fist against the foot of the Cessna's door.

"Okay, hold on."

Dale could hear the guy rummaging around up there now, looking for something. Then Tom said, "Cover your eyes. I'm gonna bust out the rest of this window."

Dale said, "Gimme a sec," and slipped down into the tub, his arm really starting to throb now. He looked at it in the poor light of his enclosure, the stake itself about as thick as his thumb, tapering to a point that was tenting the skin on the opposite side of his arm.

Fighting the urge to puke, Dale said, "Okay," and closed his eyes, less to protect them from flying glass than to stop himself from looking at his arm. He heard the glass break out there, a few shards of it raining down into his wet hair, then wiggled his good arm and head back up through the hole, thinking he was going to have to do something about that wooden spike. He glanced at the hit waiting for him on the dinner tray and knew what he would do.

Then Tom said, "Here you go," and a lime green, capsule-shaped bag came through the window. It took Dale a moment to realize it was a sleeping bag in its storage sack and he reached for it with trembling fingers, snagging one of the dangling tie strings at the limit of his reach. "It's an arctic bag," Tom said. "Slip into that puppy you'll be warm as toast in a jiffy."

Dale thought, *Fucking guy's way too cheerful.* But he eeled down into the tub again and, using his teeth as a second hand, got the sleeping bag out and wrangled his way into it, the dry fabric sticking to his wet skin. He was still freezing, but it was better.

His arm wasn't just throbbing now, it was killing him. He reached through the hole, snagged the insulin syringe off the tray and brought it down into the tub with him. The dose he'd prepared, he realized now, was a lethal one, and maybe he would've done it and maybe he wouldn't; it didn't really matter anymore. The only thing that did matter was the howling pain in his arm.

He uncapped the syringe with his teeth and injected a safe amount into a vein on the back of his hand. The rush was instantaneous, dissolving the pain like sugar in water.

Dale grinned.

Then he braced his arm against his knees, gripped the fat end of the splinter between his teeth and pulled the fucking thing out, barely feeling it but groaning at the sheer nastiness of it.

Tom said, "Are you okay?" and Dale told him about the splinter. Tom said to hang on, he had a First Aid kit, and Dale heard him rooting around in the cockpit again. Tom said he was taking a few things out for himself, then held it out the window for Dale to catch. Dale popped out of his hole and snatched the white tin kit out of thin air, pleased with himself for the artful catch. He examined the big splinter briefly, then dropped it into the tub and opened the First Aid kit on the tray. The hole in his arm was oozing blood and Dale gazed at it for a long moment, the wound reminding him of a bloody mouth. Then he got a roll of gauze out of the kit and wrapped his injured arm with it.

Above him Tom said, "There's a bottle of Advil in there too, if you need something for the pain."

Stoned, Dale grinned and said, "Thanks, man, I got it covered."

* * *

While Dale dressed his wound, Tom took a fresh look at his situation. An eight foot 2x4 had slashed its way through the side-wall of the cockpit and come to rest diagonally across his thighs, the jagged end of it rammed into the seat-back next to him, effectively wedging him in place. His seat was adjustable, like a car seat, but because his legs were so long it was already as far back as it would go. He tried to lift the board up and shimmy free that way, but the thing was in there so tight he couldn't even wiggle it. He struggled against it for a few seconds, then gave up, panic trying to claim him again.

The worst is over, he told himself. *Just stay calm.*

He took a breath and continued his survey. The radio was toast, wires and circuit boards bristling out of it, but the onboard emergency locator transmitter should still be working. It would be just a matter of time before a rescue was initiated, if it hadn't been already. Mandy would be on top of it by now, too, the poor thing probably worried sick.

He remembered his cell phone and dug it out of his coat pocket, but, as expected, there was no signal, and the battery was almost dead. He could never remember to plug the damned thing in.

He hoped Mandy could hold off going into labour until this was over.

He thought of his son, how frightened the little guy must be, his birthday almost certainly ruined. More than anything in this instant, Tom wanted to hold his son, smell his sweet smell, feel his tender warmth. Thinking of it made his eyes burn with tears. The wanting was an ache inside him.

Turning his mind to more immediate concerns, he said, "Dale, you warming up down there?"

"Yeah, I'm good."

"You alone up here?"

"Till you showed up. My ex was here before that. Bitch went out louder than you came in."

"Are you expecting anyone else?"

Dale said, "I hope not."

"What?"

"No, not expecting anyone."

"You don't happen to have a phone..."

"No phone."

"That's okay. We're still in good shape. Trenton Search and Rescue should've picked up my ELT by now."

"Say what?"

"Emergency Locater Transmitter. Sends out a distress signal on a dedicated frequency monitored by satellite and commercial aircraft. There's a search and rescue unit in Trenton out of the Forces Base down there. They'll be on it in a matter of hours. Probably dispatch a helicopter. We're as good as out of here."

Dale said, "Peachy," sounding foggy to Tom. Sounding stoned.

Tom said, "You okay, buddy?"

"I'm good, thanks for asking. And if it's all the same to you, I'm gonna cop a little quiet time down here."

A few seconds later Tom could hear the man snoring. He called out to him a couple of times, afraid the guy might be going into shock, but got no response. Knowing there was little he could do about it anyway, he retrieved the supplies he'd removed from his First Aid kit and set about cleaning and dressing the gash at his hairline.

17

WITHIN AN HOUR OF THE CRASH of Tom Stokes' Cessna 180, the signal from the ELT beacon in the tail of the aircraft was picked up by a passing satellite and transmitted to the Sat Centre in Toronto. The specifics of approximate location and type of aircraft were then passed on to Captain Dan Tremblay of the Air and Marine Search and Rescue Unit at CFB Trenton. It was Tremblay's job to dispatch the appropriate S&R aircraft, in this case a CC-130 Hercules, a four-engine fixed-wing turbo-prop that would head the search aspect of the mission, and a Bell 412 Griffon helicopter to execute the rescue.

From what Tremblay had so far been able to ascertain, the Cessna had gone down in a snow squall somewhere deep in the Kukagami region, a rugged, sprawling tourist area about 500 kilometres north of Trenton. Wild country up there, Tremblay knew, lots of lakes, rocky hills and dense forest. Summer dwellings for the most part, sparsely populated at this time of year, which meant little to no road access, especially in the more remote reaches of the region, where the Cessna was believed to have gone down. Survival in a small plane crash in terrain like that, even in good weather, was unlikely at best; but it wasn't

Tremblay's job to juggle the odds, it was to act on what he knew. And, based on the data he'd been able to procure from the Cessna's unique beacon signal, what he did know was that the plane was a commercial one, registered to an experienced operator who ran a small hunt-and-fish camp business in partnership with his wife, also an experienced pilot. The first thing he'd have to do was contact their business on Windy Lake, forty kilometres north of Sudbury, and see if anyone there could help narrow down the exact location of the aircraft.

The phone rang as he reached for it. He answered and the switchboard operator told him she had a Mrs. Mandy Stokes holding for him on line three. He punched the extension and said, "Mrs. Stokes, my name is Captain Tremblay. I was just about to call you."

18

SUMIT DROVE THE BIG MERCEDES GL with infinite care, the highway greasy from a fresh dusting of snow. Sanj sat next to him in the passenger seat, the map Ed had drawn for them open across his knees.

Five hours into their journey now and they were headed east on Highway 17 in full darkness, Indian music coming from the vehicle's state-of-the-art sound system. Sumit hummed along tunelessly, irritating the shit out of his brother.

Sanj ejected the CD and pointed through the windscreen at a blush of artificial light beyond the crest of a long hill. "That should be the gas station up there," he said. "Just past it is where we turn."

Sumit said, "Good. My heated arse is killing me."

The GL crested the hill and the brothers saw the gas station fifty metres ahead on the left. There was a convenience store annexed to the station and, tucked further back off the highway, a neon-lit bar. The parking area fronting the bar was packed with pickup trucks, SUVs and a dozen or so long-haul rigs idling in a tidy row. A few revelers stood smoking by the entrance. There were a couple of cars angle-parked in front of the convenience store and a black Dodge Ram sitting at the pump island closest to the highway.

Sumit said, "Is that Ed's truck?" and Sanj said, "Pull in."

Signaling as he slowed, Sumit turned into the farthest entryway, the GL gliding past the rear end of the Ram now, thirty feet away on their left. Through tinted glass the men saw Ronnie in profile over there, shoving the gas nozzle back into its cradle.

Sanj said, "Park around the side. If baby brother's with her, it could get messy."

As Sumit rolled to a stop in the shadow of the building's flank, Sanj turned in his seat to watch Ronnie lock the Ram with the remote, then march toward the convenience store with her bag slung over her shoulder, unzipping her jacket as she went.

Sumit killed the engine and pocketed the keys. "Think she made us?"

Sanj shook his head. "Didn't bat an eye." He gave Sumit the spare key to the Ram. "See where I'm going with this?"

Sumit smiled and got out of the Mercedes, striding across the lot now, turning up the collar of his dark Armani overcoat to hide his face.

Sanj got out to watch him go, keeping the GL between himself and the glass-walled convenience store. He watched his brother walk around the back of the Ram, the vehicle concealing him from view for a moment, then saw him climb into the back seat and hunker down out of sight.

All they had to do now was wait.

19

WHILE THE KID AT THE COUNTER STARED at her tits, Ronnie slipped a container of breath mints into her bag, then a Kit Kat bar. It still irked her that Dale had pussied out on her, but on the bright side she was half a fucking millionaire now, and mutts like Dale were a dime a dozen. It occurred to her again that if she took the time to cut and sell the shit herself she'd be a millionaire, but the truth was she didn't have the skills or the connections to get it done without risking another prison stint; she'd already done a stretch in Kingston for solicitation and had vowed never to wind up on the inside again. Better to move the product in quantity and be done with it. Ziggy could make it happen in a heartbeat; all she had to do was get to him. Crossing the border in Ed's Ram could be tricky—given Ed's past, chances were good the Feds had a line on the vehicle—but she could trade out the Ram for something else before crossing. She'd have to dress herself down a little, but if she drew the right asshole at the border, she'd be on her way to sunny Palm Beach and Ziggy's loving arms.

The kid fetched her a deck of smokes and Ronnie settled her bill in cash. She tipped the kid a wink on her way out and watched the little hard-on turn beet red. She tucked the smokes into her bag, fished out the keys and unlocked the Ram with the remote on her way across the lot, holding her coat shut against the wind.

Back in the Ram, she got a smoke out of the new deck and lit it with her Bic, almost dropping it when a familiar voice said, "Smoking in Ed's truck, I should tell him." She wheeled around to see Sumit pop up in the back seat like a slick brown jack-in-the-box, a stupid-ass grin on his face.

"Jesus Christ, Sumit," she said, "you scared the shit out me." She crushed her cigarette in the ashtray and slid her hand back into her bag, finding the pearl grip of her Colt .380 ... but before she could draw it Sanj appeared at her side window, tapping on the glass with the muzzle of a silenced semi-auto.

Ronnie powered open the window. These two fuckers showing up here could only mean one thing: Ed was going to do his own brother. That or wind up on Copeland's chopping block himself. She had little doubt that Ed had figured out who was behind the take-down with the Asians; but he'd given the responsibility to Dale, and she'd spent enough time around men like these to know about that whole bullshit code they pretended to live by. Honour among thieves. The punishment had to fall to Dale. Still, there was no way Ed was going to let her walk, and she knew that if she was going to survive this night she'd have to come up with something clever and fast.

She considered pulling the .380 anyway, do Sanj first, shoot him in the face, then double-tap Sumit through the back of her seat; but Sanj had his piece aimed at her throat now, the gun resting casually on the window sill, Sanj smiling at her like they were just hanging out. She'd let Sumit fuck her a few times back in her club days, before she hooked up with Dale, but she'd never been with Sanj.

Seeing her angle now, Ronnie returned Sanj's smile, using her left hand to tug her tank top down to show a little more cleavage, keeping her right hand, still in her bag, firmly on the Colt. She said, "I'm glad I ran into you boys. I was just bringing Ed his shit back." Turning now to look at Sumit in the back seat. "It's behind the seat back there, honey. The cash, too." She watched him turn his back on her to retrieve the stuff, saying, "Fucking Dale went psycho on those Asians. Who knew he had it in him, right? Either way, I'm done with the creep. Threw his cheesy little diamond in his face." Looking at Sanj again, showing him the ring finger of her left hand. "See?" Saying to Sanj as she pulled the .380, "Man like you's more my speed. All that brown sugar—"

Then Sanj had her by the wrist, twisting hard as he pulled her hand up with the .380 in it, taking it from her as Ronnie said, "Easy, big fella, I was just going to hand it to you. As an act of good faith."

Grinning at Sumit, Sanj said, "Good faith," and pocketed the Colt. He traced the silencer over the swells of Ronnie's breasts, the frosty steel making her shiver, saying, "You know what, though, bro? I like her. Tits *and* balls."

Then Ronnie saw Sanj signal Sumit with his eyes, twitching his gaze toward the convenience store, and Sumit got out of the vehicle. Ronnie turned her head to watch him jog to the Mercedes and stick the dope and the cash in the back seat, wondering how she'd missed it, a fucking Mercedes crossover out here in Hicksville, then felt Sanj's cold fingers on her chin, turning her to face him.

She said, "I was gonna give Ed his stuff back, Sanj. Honest. See if he could maybe put me back to work in one of the clubs—"

Sanj put a finger to her lips, then flared his coat open to

holster his gun. "I said I liked you, Ronnie, and I meant it. Unfortunately, our boss is not of a like mind." He said, "Some friendly advice? Move. Preferably to another continent."

Wary, Ronnie said, "I can go?"

"Correctly answer this skill testing question, and yes, you can go. Where's the fuckhead?"

Ronnie said, "I left him at the cottage," and glanced at the convenience store, Sumit shifting from aisle to aisle in there now, looking for Dale.

"Lover's spat?"

Looking at Sanj again, Ronnie said, "He's a dipshit."

"Is the dipshit armed?"

"That's two skill testing questions."

"Don't push it, sweetheart."

And there it was, welling up in her now, that annoying weakness for sad little boys like Dale. She lied, saying, "No, he's not armed," and was afraid Sanj had seen it.

But he said," All right," and opened her door. "Now give me the keys and get the fuck out of the vehicle."

"Shit, Sanj, are you kidding me? How am I supposed to get home? It's the middle of winter in the middle of no place."

Sanj stuck his hand out for the keys. "Not my problem. Now hand 'em over and move your ass before I change my mind."

Ronnie could see what was coming now, knew that Sanj was playing her and as soon as she set foot on the ground he'd put a bullet in her head and roll her body into the ditch or maybe dump her into the back seat and get rid of her later.

If she could just get to the guns she'd stashed under the passenger seat…

She let her bag slide off her knees into the opposite foot well, knowing how risky it was but seeing no other option—

then a big Chevy pickup rolled up to the pump island next to the Ram and Ronnie grabbed her bag by the strap and slid out the door to stand on the running board in front of Sanj, leaning over the roof to say to the redneck getting out of the pickup, "Hey, cowboy, wanna buy a lady a drink?" and saw a second redneck getting out on the passenger side, coming around the hood now to get a closer look at her.

Sanj put his hand inside his coat and Ronnie dropped the keys into the slush at his feet, hopping down to scoot past him and put the redneck between herself and Sanj.

The redneck said, "Who's the raghead?"

Ronnie said, "Carwash guy," and took the creep's arm, hustling him toward the bar. Watching it happen, the first redneck said, "Hey, man, the lady was talking to me," and Ronnie said, "Don't worry, boys, there's plenty to go around."

Then she was in the parking area, fifty feet and a tight row of vehicles between her and Sanj, the sick fuck bending over now to pick up the keys. At the entrance to the bar she stopped to watch Sanj park the Ram on the far side of the convenience store and lock it with the remote, then get into the Mercedes and drive it to the front of the store to pick up Sumit. She watched him slide over to the passenger side as Sumit came out of the store to get behind the wheel.

The redneck asked her what she was drinking and Ronnie ignored him long enough to see the Mercedes accelerate up the road leading in to the cottage. Then she said, "Whatever you're buyin', big fella," and followed him into the bar.

* * *

Sumit said, "You let her go?"

"Cagey bitch gave me the slip."

Smiling, Sumit said, "Be a shame to put a hole in that, anyway. Get her hot, the girl tastes like apricots." He said, "What do we tell Ed?"

"We never saw her."

"How much further?"

Sanj switched on the dome light to check the map, then said, "About an hour."

Sumit said, "Fucking shit detail," and turned the CD player back on, resuming the Indian music.

"Enough of that shit," Sanj said. "Find me some rock and roll before I die."

20

DALE CAME OUT OF HIS NOD to the urgent sound of his name—
"Dale? Dale!—and once again had to muddle through a narcotic
haze to bring fully to mind the jackpot he'd got himself into.
Cozy in the thermal bag down in the tub, he said, "What's up?"

"I thought I heard something on the roof of the plane. Can
you see anything?"

Dale said, "Gimme a sec," and poked his head through the
gap in the debris. He looked up at the plane and at first could see
nothing. He was about to say as much when he heard something
shift up there, far enough around the curve of the fuselage that
he couldn't see what it was. A soft padding sound...

Then he was staring into the bright amber eyes of a cougar,
the cat edging forward to peer down at him over the flank of the
plane.

Dale said, "There's a fucking cougar right behind you," and
got Trang's gun off the dinner tray.

Tom said, "Are you serious?"

"As a train wreck."

"How's it look?"

"Hungry."

No, I mean how does it *look*? Curious? Angry? Afraid?"

Dale said, "Hungry," and aimed the gun at the big cat's head. "I'm gonna shoot him."

"Jesus, no," Tom said. "Don't even *look* at him. If you shoot and miss, we're dead."

"Yeah, and if I shoot and don't miss, he's fucking dead."

"Are you a good shot?"

Dale looked at his trembling hand. "Never shot a gun in my life." He said, "Oh, shit, he's coming right at you," and aimed again at the sleek wildcat, the animal shifting its body into full view now.

Dale pulled the trigger and nothing happened. Not even a click. He looked at the gun, then up at the cougar as it leaned over to sniff the edge of the broken window in Tom's door, then stuck its head inside.

* * *

Tom looked up into the cat's vivid face, less than a foot from his own now. Dale had been right: it looked hungry, winter lean and slavering.

Tom leaned away from it as much as he could, which wasn't very far, and now the animal snarled, baring a set of savage yellow incisors as long as Tom's pinkie and twice as thick, the vapour of its breath reeking of rot and death.

Taking its time, the big cat bit experimentally into the shoulder of Tom's coat, catching only the fabric. It tugged and Tom said, "Son of a—"

* * *

Dale found the safety and flipped it off, aimed the gun at the cougar again and squeezed the trigger.

Click!

What the fuck?

The cat had its head all the way in the window now and Dale thought of the hundreds of action movies he'd seen. He thought, *Rack the fucking slide* and dragged himself down into the tub again, using his free hand to chamber a round. Then he was back up through the hole, watching the animal brace its feet to pull at something up there. He heard Tom say, "Son of a—" aimed and pulled the trigger with his eyes closed, the gun kicking in his hand as he discharged five or six rounds, the sharp reports popping his ears. When he opened his eyes the cougar was gone. Like magic.

Tom said, "Did you get him?" and stuck his finger through a bullet hole in the door of the plane. "'Cause you damned near got me."

Dale said, "Holy fuck he's gone. Did you see that bastard?"

"*See* him. I've got his *teeth* marks in my coat."

"Jesus Christ, Tommy, what a day."

"You got that right," Tom said. "What next?"

And both men were caught in that crazed laughter again.

21

SANJ POINTED THROUGH THE WINDSCREEN at a reflective green road sign. "Cottage Road," he said. "Turn right up here."

Sumit slowed to make the turn, shifting the Mercedes into four-wheel drive.

"Three more miles of this shit," Sanj said, "and we're there."

Turning the radio down, Sumit said, "So last night I'm having drinks at the Tryst, this woman, she's got to be fifty—but classy, well-put-together—bitch comes out of nowhere and tells me her name is Crystal and if I buy her a Mai Tai she'll give me a night I'll never forget."

Sanj said, "More like a disease you'll never forget."

"Didn't strike me as the type. Looking at her, I'm thinking newly divorced or maybe she caught her old man boning the help. Anyway, it's late, I've got a glow on, but she's almost as old as Maa so I tell her no, but in a nice way, polite. She gives me a pouty look and catches me scoping that fine big ass as she's walking away. Throws a little smile over her shoulder and keeps on going."

Sanj said, "Wait, you're actually considering it at this point?"

"Fuck, no, man. I'm just playing with her. I've never slept with a woman older than twenty-five."

"What about that Japanese beauty last summer, remember? Broadzilla? You're late, Ed's waiting outside, I walk in and there you are on the bed with this skank's got to be forty, has more hair on her ass than you."

"Fucking Saki, man, fucks you up. Where I met her it was dark."

"Keep telling yourself that, little brother."

"You take that video off your phone like I told you?"

"Make me late again you can watch it on YouTube."

"Assrag."

"So'd you do the MILF or not?"

"Why should I tell you?"

"Because you want to."

Grinning, Sumit said, "So a half hour goes by, I'm paying my tab and here she comes again, stoked to the gills now, and tells me if I drive her home there's a mother-daughter tag team in it for me. Says it's all arranged."

"Now we're getting somewhere."

"Her apartment's just a couple blocks away so I drive her, we go inside, she flips on the light and shouts up the stairs, 'Mom, you still up?'"

Sanj laughed and said, "Please tell me you didn't go for it..." but then the road dead-ended and both men fell mute.

Sumit brought the Mercedes around and switched on the high beams, fixing the light on the lake-facing side of the cottage, Sumit saying, "Is that a fucking plane?"

22

Dale said, "You hear that?"

Tom said, "I bet that's our rescue. See? I told you we'd be all right."

"One vehicle?" Dale said, getting a bad feeling. "Weren't you talking about helicopters and shit?"

"Maybe they sent in the local police. What difference does it make?"

Tom started to rustle around in the cockpit and Dale said, "*Shh*. Listen…"

The slam of a car door now, followed by another, then a voice that made Dale's skin crawl, Sumit the psychopath saying, "It *is* a fucking plane."

Lowering his voice, Dale said to Tom, "Don't say a word. Don't even breathe. These guys are stone killers and they're here for me."

Moving fast, Dale grabbed the gun off the dinner tray and squirmed down into the tub with it, then popped back up for the rest of his stuff, getting it all out sight.

He heard Tom say, "What's going on?" and scrunched himself down as far as he could into the foot of the tub, just managing to squirm around onto his elbows and knees under the fuselage, keeping the gun aimed at the hole in the debris. He said, "Play dead, okay? If they come anywhere near you, just play dead."

"But—"

"*Just do it.*"

23

MANDY SNUGGED STEVE'S COVERS across his chest, the little guy lying flat on his back in bed, so worried about his dad he forgot his teddy on the chair, so exhausted he could barely keep his eyes open. His party had been a wash, the poor kid sitting on Mandy's lap in front of the radio until his guests finally gave up and went home. He hadn't opened a single gift, telling her he'd do it when his dad got home because it was his birthday, too. It wasn't until she promised to wake him as soon as she heard anything that he'd finally agreed to come up to bed.

She got his teddy off the chair and tucked it under his arm, then sat next to him on the bed, offering one last reassurance as she stroked his hair. "Try not to worry, sweetie," she told him. "Your daddy's a good pilot. I'm sure he just landed to get out of the storm and the weather's messing up the radio. It's happened before."

"The rescue team is looking for him?"

"They sure are," Mandy said, and kissed him on the tip of his turned-up nose. "I already talked to them, remember? They said they'd have news for us soon." She kissed him again. "Try to sleep now, okay? When you wake up, this will all be over."

But the boy was already fast asleep.

As Mandy stood, she got a fresh jab of pain low in her abdomen and her fingers went to it instinctively, pressing as if to extinguish it, and after a moment it was gone.

In the kitchen she poured herself a mug of stale coffee, then returned to the radio in front of the picture window, as black now as the night that pressed against it.

24

SANJ SAID, "LOOK AT THIS MESS."

They stood staring at the wreckage in the wash of the GL's
high beams, the aircraft's tail section jutting out through the
window, the severed wings and skis lying twisted against the
foot of the building.

"Unreal," Sumit said. "You're sure this is the right place?"

"According to the map. Ronnie didn't mention it, so it
must've just happened."

"Doesn't look like the kind of thing you walk away from,"
Sumit said. "Maybe we got lucky and it clipped Ed's asshole
brother for us."

"Give Ed his bullet back."

"Lights are still on in there," Sumit said, drawing his weapon.
"Shall we?"

Sanj pulled his silenced 9mm and followed Sumit to the
front door. Sumit turned the knob and the door swung open on
silent hinges. They took up positions on either side of the frame
for a long moment, listening, then Sumit stepped inside, bringing his gun to bear. Sanj moved in behind him, stepping around
him now to get the lay of the land.

The place was small, the lit foyer leading into a hallway that ran parallel to the side of the building the plane had come through, the hallway itself opening onto what looked like a kitchenette on the left and a sitting area on the right. There was a single closed door halfway down on the right, the lights on in there, a film of snow and plaster dust on the floor in front of it, blown there through the crack under the door.

Sanj pointed at the door and Sumit nodded. Sumit stepped past him and kicked the door open, snapping it off its top hinge, shifting fast out of the opening to press his back to the adjacent wall. Sanj took a quick look inside, scanning for targets, then relaxed, holstering his weapon. "Shitter," he said. "Looks clear."

Sumit followed him into the bathroom, both men pausing to take in the scene: the room trashed, the front third of the plane's fuselage resting across the rims of the tub, snow blowing in from the window ten feet away on the other side of the demolished wall. No signs of life.

Sumit said, "Shouldn't we check the rest of the place?"

"Forget it," Sanj said. "He's long gone. The bitch must've made us and told him to hide in the store."

"I checked the store. No way he was in there."

"Then he spotted us and ducked out the back," Sanj said. "Either way, he's in the wind." He stepped up onto the edge of the tub, straddling it now to look into the cockpit. "There's a guy in here."

"Is he dead?"

"Who am I, House? He looks dead. Blood on his face."

"Check his pulse."

Sanj had to yank hard on the door to get it halfway open, the door binding against the bent frame, then he reached in and felt the guy's neck. The guy moaned and Sanj flinched back, saying,

"Holy shit, he's alive," then said to the guy in the plane, "Hey, man, are you okay?"

* * *

Tom gripped his emergency flare gun, holding it out of sight between the seats, but he wasn't sure if he should use it. All he had to go on was what Dale had said about these guys, and if Dale was wrong he'd be shooting at one of his rescuers with a live flare. And if Dale was right...well, there were two of them, and while bringing a flare gun to a gunfight might be better than bringing a knife, it was still no hell against seasoned killers.

He let the flare gun slip quietly to the cockpit floor and pretended to come to, bringing his head around to face a young East Indian guy leaning over him with an expression of concern, the guy smelling of cologne, no hint of threat about him. Still, the fear in Dale's voice had been very real and, either way, Tom believed he had a plan that could defuse the situation and get them both out of here alive.

He acted dazed for a moment, like he didn't know where he was, then drew a panicked breath and the guy touched his shoulder, saying, "Hey, friend, calm down. Your plane crashed but I think you're okay."

"I must've blacked out," Tom said. "Is this your place? I've been yelling for help for a while now. Thought I was going to die up here."

Assessing Tom's situation, the guy said, "Shit, man, you're really wedged in there, aren't you." He leaned in and tried to shift the stud off Tom's thighs—giving Tom a close-up view of the handgun holstered under his arm—but couldn't get it to budge.

Now the guy turned to face the room, saying, "Get up here

and give me a hand," and Tom felt the fuselage shift as a second East Indian popped up to find his footing on the rims of the tub.

Tom was a lapsed Catholic, but he prayed that neither of these guys fell through the shelf of debris that hid Dale from view. If that happened, it would be the end of them both.

As the men tried to free him, Tom said, "Sorry about your place. I'm fully insured."

"I wouldn't worry about it," the first guy said. "Let's just get you out of there."

With one guy working from outside the aircraft, gripping the butt end of the stud where it came through the fuselage, and the other reefing on the section across Tom's thighs, the board started to move, wood screeching against metal until Tom was able to shimmy his legs out from under and bunch himself into a squat in his seat, feeling like he might black out now for real.

The first guy backed out of the doorway and lost his balance, shifting his foot back to brace himself as the second guy reached out to steady him. The first guy said, "Shit," and Tom saw his bracing foot punch through the overlapping layers of debris, sinking to the ankle before the second guy had him. Tom thought of grabbing the flare gun again, but now both men were laughing about it, the first one leaning on the other to pull his foot free.

Then they were helping Tom down from the wreckage, the second guy looking at him like he was a celebrity, saying to his partner, "We should take this guy to the track with us, man. He is one lucky son of a bitch."

Tom let the men take his weight until his feet were flat on the bathroom floor, then he leaned against a section of undamaged wall, waiting for the circulation to return to his legs and flush out the numbness.

The first guy stood right in front of Tom now, getting in his space, not laughing anymore. "So you didn't see anyone else?" he said.

"Not a soul," Tom said, favouring his right leg, pretending he was hurt. He said, "Would you guys mind calling me an ambulance? I think my leg might be broken."

The first guy said, "Sumit, give me a hand with this guy." Then to Tom: "Don't worry. We'll take you into the city."

That was when Dale popped out of his hole and started shooting.

* * *

His first two rounds slammed into Sumit, killing him instantly. He fired next at Sanj, seeing Tom in his peripheral vision diving for cover, but the shots went over Sanj's head as the man crouched to draw his weapon. Dale followed him down, but Trang's gun was empty now, the slide locked open, gunsmoke wisping from the muzzle.

Sanj rose from his crouch, the 9mm aimed at Dale's face, then bent to feel Sumit's wrist for a pulse, even though it was clear the man was dead.

"Something you may not know about Sumit," Sanj said to Dale with an eerie calm, rising to his full height. "He's my baby brother. Apart from Ed, you're the only person in this country I've ever told that to. Even Copeland has no idea. Given the nature of our work, we thought it best to keep our relationship private." He glanced again at Sumit's body. "And now you've killed him. Fitting, I suppose, even ironic, considering the task Ed sent us here to complete."

While the maniac talked, Dale felt around in the tub for the splinter that had pierced his arm, knowing it wouldn't do him any good but believing he'd feel better about dying with a weapon in his hand. His fingers fell instead on an empty syringe and he wished he could do one last hit, the drug his only refuge from a life that had never fit him. He saw Tom on his feet behind Sanj now, pressed against the wall in fear, and felt a dull regret for the man, with his wife and kid and another one on the way, all of that gone now. Sanj would leave no loose ends.

Dale braced for the bullet he knew was coming, but then the crazy fucker holstered his gun and drew a switchblade from his belt, the *snick* of the blade making Dale's skin crawl as Sanj moved toward him.

Sanj said, "Your brother told me to make it quick and pain-less. Fuck him."

Then Sanj lunged and Dale threw Trang's gun at him and tried to squirm down into the tub, but Sanj caught him by the wrist and pulled him back up, sweeping the blade toward his neck. "No you don't, you little—"

And Tom hit the man in the back of the head with a broken stud, the sound like a baseball being struck, Sanj slamming to the tile floor like a felled tree.

The two men stared at each other for a long moment, Dale in his hole, Tom standing over the bodies, then Tom tossed the board aside and knelt next to Sanj, feeling his neck for a pulse. "Oh, Jesus. I think I killed him. I fucking killed him…"

Dale whooped. "Fuck him, Tommy, you saved my *life*."

Startling Dale, Tom rose up and bellowed at him: "It's *Tom*. And why the *fuck* didn't you stay out of sight? I had them out of here."

"Don't even sweat that piece of shit, Tom. These pricks have killed more people than cancer. It was us or them."

"I had them out of here."

"Look, it's done. Nothing we can do about it now. Help me out of this gopher hole and we'll take their vehicle."

"Oh, no. No way. We're going to wait right here for the rescue team and when they get here you're going to tell them exactly what happened. This is your fucking mess, not mine. I've got a family, a new baby on the way. I can't go to jail."

"Tom, listen to me. You don't know me from Adam, right? But we've been through the ringer together here. If I don't get out of here, and I mean right now, I'm a dead man." He took a deep breath, desperate to make this man understand. "My ex, she killed some guys, stole some stuff, but they're blaming it on me."

Tom said, "If it wasn't your fault, you'll have police protection."

"They got the cops on their payroll. Trust me, my only chance is to vanish."

"And what about me?" Tom said, pointing at the wreckage. "That's *my* plane. No way to hide that. How do I explain all this?"

Dale was silent for a moment...then he had it. "You tell them this was the way you found the place. Whatever happened, happened *before* you crashed. You found the bodies, helped yourself to the keys and got the fuck out of here. Who wouldn't?" Dale could see him considering it and said, "It'll work. You get me to a bus station on your way home, I'm in Mexico before my brother even finds out these bastards are deceased."

"Your brother?"

"It's a long story. I'll tell you all about it on the way. Now please, get me *out* of here."

Tom picked up the 2x4 he'd struck Sanj with and wedged it under the fuselage, using the rim of the tub as a fulcrum. He heaved on it and the aircraft shifted enough for Dale to clear some of the debris and wriggle out of his bolt hole.

Tom saw him standing there naked, shivering in the cold, and looked away, saying, "I must be insane. But we're going to my place first. My wife and son must be worried to death."

Dale said, "Whatever you say." He pulled the sleeping bag out of the tub and draped it over his shoulders. Then he squatted next to the bodies, taking the guns and the keys for the Mercedes. He jingled the keys at Tom. "We're set," he said. "Just let me find my clothes."

* * *

Tom followed Dale out of the bathroom, not wanting to be left alone with the dead brothers in their overcoats. He remembered it was his birthday and felt that hysterical laughter welling up in him again, except this time it wasn't about escaping death, it was about causing one. When he'd swung that 2x4 he'd intended only to knock the man out, then tie him up and let the cops deal with him; but as he wound up for the strike, something snapped almost audibly in his brain and he backed the swing with every ounce of force he could muster, a flat and fierce voice inside him saying *Kill him*; and no matter how he felt about it now, that was what he'd wanted, to kill this man who'd come into his life through no fault of his own and would almost certainly have taken the knife to him when he got finished with Dale. And if a plane crash hadn't managed to take him away from his family, there was no way he was going to allow that shark-eyed motherfucker to do it. No way.

Still, he'd killed a man, and in the aftermath of the act he thought he might vomit. He slouched into a chair in the kitchenette while Dale got his clothes on, wanting only to get home, get back to his wife and son and hold onto them for dear life.

Dale was standing over him now, fully dressed, resting a

hand on his shoulder, saying, "You okay, Tom? You're white as a ghost."

Yeah," Tom said. "Yeah, yeah, I'm fine." He got to his feet, his legs still wobbly from the motionless hours in the cockpit. "Ready to go?"

"Yeah, man, let's book."

* * *

The winter air felt good against Tom's skin and he unzipped his jacket to let more of it in. The worst of the storm had passed, and now the moon shone through a rent in the cloud cover, its silver light showing him the ruts in the embankment from the Cessna's skis, showing him the tail section of the aircraft framed in the window and leaving him to wonder how in the name of God he'd survived.

Walking to the Mercedes, Dale said, "Man, did you ever clip that crazy fucker. Caved that thick skull all the way in. I've always hated those guys."

Tom said, "Give me the keys," and Dale did.

They climbed into the GL, the cab still warm from the drive in, and the engine turned over on the first try.

Dale said, "We're golden."

Tom said, "Don't talk to me, okay?"

"I can do that."

Head throbbing, Tom steered the Mercedes onto the road, thinking only about getting home.

25

SANJ BELIEVED HE WAS DEAD.

He felt as cold as the dead, numb and detached from himself, and it made him think of how foolish he'd been all these years to dismiss out of hand the possibility of life after death.

Reincarnation.

Was that where he was now? In the midst of his transformation?

He remembered his grandmother telling him scary stories of bad little boys coming back as cockroaches and gutter rats....

But could the dead feel pain? Like the metreed throbbing in his skull?

He remembered being struck and thinking as his legs gave out that he had never in his life been hit so *hard*, the blow feeling mortal.

He thought, *My fucking head,* and sent a command to his body to *move*, but the command was ignored. Even his eyelids refused to obey.

Now he heard a noise, a dragging sound, and a harsh rasp of breath. His own, yes, but that of another as well, rapid and strained.

Demon or god?

With what seemed like a gargantuan effort, Sanj opened his eyes. It took him a few seconds to bring the world into focus, then he saw that he was lying face down on the tile floor—Ed's brother shooting Sumit, the crashed plane, the pilot coldcocking him with a piece of lumber, all of it coming back to him now—then he registered movement at the edge of his vision.

He shifted his head and saw Sumit's python-skin cowboy boots jerking past his face with Sumit still in them. He raised his gaze and saw Sumit's head slung forward on his chest, a cougar with blazing yellow eyes tugging him inch by inch through the doorway, its teeth buried to the gum line in Sumit's shoulder.

Sanj slid his hand down to his ankle and unholstered his backup piece, raised it in a grip that was weak and unsteady and jerked the trigger. The slug went wide and the flat report panicked the wildcat, the animal turning tail and darting out of sight. Sanj held his aim for a while, smelling that gamey reek of damp pelt, then let the gun sink to the floor.

After a while he managed to get to his feet, feeling the boggy wet split in his scalp, seeing the blood on his fingers, and steadied himself against the vanity. When his head was clear enough he went down on one knee to kiss his brother's forehead, then rolled him out of his overcoat and covered him with it. "I'm sorry, little brother," he said.

Then he climbed back onto the wreckage.

26

THE IDIOTS IN THE PICKUP TRUCK were cousins, both of them welders who came in here every night to get shitfaced and take a run at the local poon, which, from what Ronnie had seen tonight, couldn't be much of a challenge. She let the boys buy her a drink because she needed one, then told them she was going to powder her nose, which she did, sitting in a stall that stunk of piss and cheap perfume to snort a few lines of coke. Cocaine was her ON switch and Ronnie surrendered herself to it now, holding her breath as the drug sketched a course of action in her mind. When it was vividly clear, she came out of the stall at a brisk march, heels clocking the filthy floor, the half-dozen skanks preening at the mirror shrinking away from her.

She shouldered her way through the drunks on the dance floor and went outside with her coat open, heading for the convenience store. She saw a long-handled ice scraper leaning by the front door and seized it without breaking stride.

Sanj had parked the Ram well back in the shadow of the building, and Ronnie walked around to the passenger-side window and used the ice scraper to smash the glass, getting most of it with her first swing. She leaned the scraper against the truck and reached in to unlock the door.

The guns she'd taken off the Asians were still under the seat and she stuffed them into her bag. Then she used the scraper to shatter every window in the Ram, just for the hell of it. From a secret pocket in her bag she took out a folding knife with a 4-inch Bowie blade and used it to puncture the sidewalls of all four tires, the hiss of compressed air and the smell of expensive rubber making her laugh out loud. "Take that back to your boss," she said. "Cocksuckers."

Then she returned to the bar. She needed a new set of wheels.

27

SANJ UNCLIPPED A PHOTOGRAPH from the sun visor in the cockpit, an image of an attractive blonde woman—early thirties, natural looking—pushing a dark-haired boy of maybe four on a backyard swing set: the pilot's family, Sanj knew. He flipped the shot over and read the inscription, written in an elegant script: *With love, Mandy and Steve.*

He found a flat leather pouch behind the visor with the man's pilot license in it, his name—Tom Stokes—and the address of his aviation business, which, Sanj could see now, was also where the fucker lived.

He tucked the photo and the pouch into his coat pocket. He noticed a bunch of keys hanging from the ignition and took those, too.

He got to the floor and sat on the edge of the tub, his head pounding, blood still trickling from his scalp wound. He felt foggy, the pain making it difficult to think. He had to determine how he was getting out of here... but his gaze kept drifting to his brother's body, lying there under his coat. They had no family in this country, their parents both dead, and the rest—aunts, uncles, cousins—all back in India and long since estranged. There was

no one that cared whether they lived or died. No one but himself
and a few sullen criminals to attend Sumit's funeral.

Still, he hated to leave his brother like this, so exposed.
Every time he blinked he saw that cougar trying to drag Sumit's
body out to feast on later, like Sumit was an animal instead of
the smartest, funniest, most fiercely loyal human being Sanj had
ever had the privilege of knowing. And by far the craziest.

He bent over Sumit's body and started going through his
pockets, making sure there was nothing left on him the cops
could use to identify him. When he found Sumit's cell phone he
checked it for a signal, then did the same with his own, but there
was nothing on either one.

An idea of such perfection came to him then that he knew
Sumit would approve: he'd siphon some gas from the plane and
use it set the building on fire, destroying any evidence, keeping
that fucking wildcat at bay, and giving his brother a proper cre-
mation all at the same time. And even this far out in the boonies
a blaze of such size would almost certainly attract some attention, providing him with a ride home.

He found a length of clear plastic tubing in a storage closet
by the back door. There was an empty five gallon gas can in
there, too, and Sanj brought both items back to the bathroom.

As he siphoned the gas, he remembered the years he and his
brother had spent living on the streets in the holy city of Vara-
nasi after their parents died—ironically, in a small-plane crash.
Their father was a chest surgeon, their mother a nurse, and
they'd been flying out to do some missionary work when they
got caught in a typhoon and the plane was lost in the jungle.
Their parents had been wealthy, but had disowned their two
sons when they were still in their early teens, just months before
the accident. "If you want to run wild in the streets," their father

had told them the last time they saw him alive, "you can live in the streets, too." It was Sumit who'd kept them going. Fearless, resourceful, violent Sumit.

He remembered the funeral pyres burning on the banks of the Ganges, each blaze tended by a rail-thin man in a white dhoti sitting on his haunches, using a long bamboo pole to prod the sizzling corpse, the man standing every once in a while to restack the burning logs with his pole or to slam it down on the half-incinerated body, shattering the skull or splintering the long-bones, sending up plumes of red embers and greasy smoke. He recalled the stench of burning flesh, the sizzle and pop of human fat and Sumit saying how the smell always put him in the mood for barbeque.

He'd have to stay well back from the fire once it got going. He didn't think he could bear the smell of his own brother cooking in here.

Maybe he'd light up Mandy and her brat once he caught up with them, do it in front of the pilot, see if the smell put that blindsiding chickenshit in the mood for barbeque.

When the gas can was full, he removed the hose and let the fuel continue to drain from the aircraft into a spreading puddle on the floor. He stepped over his brother and made his way through the remains of the cottage, sloshing the gas on anything that looked like it would burn: couch, curtains, throw rugs, a worn-out easy chair.

Sanj wasn't a smoker, but he found some wooden matches strewn by the open hearth. He struck a couple on the decorative rockwork but couldn't get a flame, the match heads damp from sitting out in the open. He thought of Sumit's lighter, always in his right-hand coat pocket, and retrieved it without looking at his brother's face; he didn't want to remember him this way.

The lighter was a tarnished Harley Davidson Zippo Sanj had given him for his birthday when they were kids; he'd stolen it from a street vendor who'd seen him take it and had given chase, screaming after him in some mountain dialect Sanj didn't understand, swinging a rusty old machete over his head. Crazy fucker probably would have chopped off his hand if he'd caught him.

It took a couple of tries, the wind gusting through the shattered walls to snuff the eager flame, but then he had it.

Cupping the flame with his free hand, Sanj bent to ignite his brother's gas soaked overcoat—then he heard something that stopped him cold.

Helicopter rotors.

With a last glance at Sumit's body, motionless on the cold tile floor, Sanj made his way back to the living area, the chop of rotors much louder now, their hurricane force pelting him with ice crystals as he squinted through the demolished picture window to watch the aircraft ease into a hover not fifty feet away. As it began it's descent to the frozen surface of the lake, floodlights blazed into life on its underbelly, bathing the spirals of snow it raised in a harsh noon glare.

In bold red letters on the chopper's flank was all the information Sanj needed: RESCUE.

He had his ride out of here.

28

RONNIE GOT BACK TO THE BAR in time to see the younger of the welder cousins leading a hunched platinum blond twice his age into the men's room, the two of them grinning like they shared some delicious secret. She found the other cousin, the one with the truck keys, pouting over his beer at the bar, the man lighting up like a carnival ride when he saw her approach.

"Hey, sweetlips," he said, already slurring. "Thought you run out on me."

"Now why would I do a thing like that?" Ronnie said, cozying up next to him on the stool, thinking, *Scrawny redneck, smells like mouse shit.* She turned her gaze on the men's room door. "Looks like cuz's gonna get his wick wet," she said and almost gagged when the asshole laughed, wafting the reek of digesting beer and tooth decay into her face. She said, "Cunt looks like a long stretch of rough road, though, don't she?" and the dummy nodded. "Play your cards right, you're gonna do one hell of a lot better."

"Do tell?"

"Well, call me a cowgirl—sorry, Cuz, your name again?"

"Ricky, but everybody calls me 'Grinch.'"

"Well, Ricky, call me a cowgirl, but I just love ridin' bronco in a big shiny pickup truck. What are your thoughts?"

The shitkicker almost knocked her over getting off the stool. "Couldn't agree more," he said, digging in his jeans for the keys. "Love the feel of genuine Chevy leather on my bare ass." He slapped a twenty on the bar and jingled the keys at her, saying, "Follow me."

* * *

Ricky wanted to get right into it in the parking lot, but Ronnie told him she had a better idea. "Why don't we take a ride up that country road over there? What's it called?"

"Kukagami?"

"That's the one. I've always wanted to do it on the hood of a rig like this, and for that we're gonna need some privacy."

Ricky grinned, showing those dank, snaggle teeth of his. "You crazy, girl? It's colder'n a witch's tit out there. Man'd freeze his balls off inside a minute, not to mention the shrinkage."

Ronnie curled her fingers around the door handle, saying, "Well, if you're not up for it…"

"Hey, now, sweetheart," Ricky said, grabbing her arm, "let's not be hasty," and Ronnie released the door handle. He reached past her to open the glove box and brought out an unopened pint of Wild Turkey. "Couple drags on this'll warm us right up."

He drained off more than half the contents in a pull, offered the dregs to Ronnie, who refused, then started the engine, resting the bottle in the v of his crotch. The truck's big mill rumbled as the redneck guided it to the shoulder and then out onto the highway. A minute later they were rolling smoothly along the abandoned Kukagami Road.

"Remote as fuck back here," Ricky said, squinting through

the windscreen into the glare of incoming snowflakes. Ronnie told him to turn off his brights and Ricky said, "Oh, yeah," and obeyed, saying, "Yeah, that's better." He got into the Wild Turkey again, not bothering to offer it to Ronnie this time, then cracked his window to toss out the empty. "How far up here you wanna go? This fucker goes on for miles. We get in here too deep and run into trouble…"

"Few more minutes," Ronnie said, watching for a sideroad or a plowed entryway to pull into. Signs of year-round habitation were scarce along here, just the occasional farm nestled back from the road, the surrounding fields blanketed in snow.

They drove in silence for another five minutes or so, Ronnie thinking about how she was going to play this. She didn't want to kill this happy asshole if she didn't have to, but it was an option. She'd get him out of the vehicle, then decide.

There were no sign of life at all now, just sparse bush and scrubby fields, and Ronnie said, "Is this road the only way in or out from all the summer places?"

"Uh huh. We're not gonna see another soul back here now. Look, why don't we just—"

"Right up here's good," Ronnie said, pointing at a narrow, snow-choked sideroad. "This bad boy handle the terrain?"

Ricky grinned. "I could drive this puppy cross-country through three feet of snow if I wanted. You seen the rubber on her?"

"That's great, Ricky. Now park your truck and whip out your dick."

That earned her a drunken *Woot!* that filled the cab with the stink of him and Ronnie thought, *Maybe I should kill him so he never has kids.*

Ricky stopped the truck twenty feet into the sideroad and

shifted into PARK, letting the engine idle. "You sure we gotta do this outside?" he said. "Nice and cozy in here. We got music…" He turned the radio on, already tuned to a Country & Western station, Johnny Cash doing "Ghost Riders in the Sky," the bass set so heavy on the thing it made her teeth rattle.

Ronnie turned the radio off and got out of the truck, drawing one of the guns from her purse as she bumped the door shut with her hip. Grumbling, Ricky got out, too, leaving the truck running, which meant she wouldn't have to worry about getting the keys off him.

As he came around the hood she pointed the gun at him. At first he kept right on coming, too drunk to see the threat, maybe, or thinking it was just another weird kink in the game. Then Ronnie fired a shot past his ear and Ricky sobered right up.

He stood stock still and put his hands in the air. "But you said…"

"Don't worry about what I said. Now get those clothes off, Ricky boy. All of 'em. I wanna see nothing but flesh."

He gave her a tentative grin. "Are we still gonna…?"

Ronnie said, "What's your best guess?" and Ricky undressed with renewed dexterity. Amusing her a little, he folded everything neatly onto the hood of the truck.

Butt naked now, cupping his little turtle head with both hands, he said, "You're not gonna shoot me. Are you?"

"Haven't decided yet," Ronnie said. "Why don't you show me how fast you can run." She pointed into a stand of bush on the far side of Kukagami Lake Road, a thirty-foot sprint to the trees. "Make it into those trees before I count to five and I won't shoot you."

Ricky had a quick look at the treeline, still not convinced she was serious. He said, "You mean—?"

"One..."

Ricky took off running, bare feet skidding like claws on lino-leum, arms madly pinwheeling...but somehow he managed to stay on his feet. When Ronnie said "Five," he was three feet from the trees and Ronnie took aim across the hood and shot him in the ass, laughing out loud as the poor dummy yelped, grabbed his skinny shank and kept right on running, the dark of the bush swallowing him whole a few seconds later.

She waited a moment, listening, watching to see if he'd double back, then scooped his clothes off the hood and climbed into the truck on the driver's side.

Ricky was right; the vehicle handled beautifully in the snow. Ten minutes later she was back at the convenience store with a full tank of gas and a sweet ride home.

But the more she thought about those two raghead sons of bitches grabbing her score, the more pissed off she got. Sick fuckers would've killed her, too, given the chance...

She parked the Chevy in the unlit access lane behind the store, switched the headlights off and let the engine idle. She tuned the radio to Sudbury's Best Rock, Q92, and eased her seat all the way back, getting comfy. From here she had an unob-structed view of the intersection of Kukagami Lake Road and the highway.

All she had to do now was wait.

29

NAVIGATING THE UNPLOWED COTTAGE ROAD had been slow going, but out here on Kukagami Lake Road Tom was able to lean a little harder on the Mercedes. It was a brilliant piece of engineering, and under different circumstances he might have enjoyed the way it hugged the curves and switchbacks in spite of the ice-scabbed blacktop, the comfy heated seats and almost soundproof interior.

What he *was* enjoying, however, in a sweetly perverse way, was Dale's obvious discomfort with his driving; the guy was clutching the armrests like a kid on his first roller coaster ride.

"Something bothering you?" Tom said, unable to suppress a grin. "You haven't blinked in eight miles."

"I thought I wasn't supposed to talk," Dale said through clenched teeth, uttering a startled "*Jesus*," when the rear end slewed and Tom jockeyed the wheel to correct for it.

"That was back when I wanted to kill you," Tom said. "Since then I've calmed down a fair bit." This was not untrue. With each mile he put between himself and the cottage, the easier he was finding it to replace the extreme tension of the experience with the simple excitement of seeing his family again. He couldn't remember yearning for them more. And that last patch of black ice had sobered him; he'd come uncomfortably close to taking the ditch.

He decided his life had been in peril enough for one day and backed off on the accelerator. In truth, there was no rush. He'd call home the first chance he got.

Dale blinked, blew air through his nose and loosened his grip on the armrests. After a beat of silence he said, "Tom, listen, I'm sorry I got you into this mess. Really. You're a good shit."

"Well, I did drop in kind of unexpectedly."

"You got that right," Dale said with a nervous laugh. "Still, I feel like I owe you an explanation."

Now it was Tom's turn to laugh. "You think?"

"How much time have we got?"

"More than I'd like. Another half hour to the highway, then two hours home."

"My older brother Ed brought me in," Dale said, heaving a sigh. "I met Ronnie through him…"

And over the next twenty minutes he told it all, starting with some background on his brother and Randall Copeland, then rushing through the massacre at the take-out joint to Ronnie almost shooting a cop on the drive up here before stranding him at the cottage, wrapping it all up with Tom's plane coming through the wall and almost drowning him. He paused only to field the occasional question from Tom, who listened intently and, in spite of himself, felt a twinge of sympathy for this lost, immature but clearly intelligent young man whom sheer, conscienceless chance had thrust into his life.

Wrapping it up, Dale said, "But you know what? I'm glad you showed up. Because you saved my life. Twice."

"What do you mean, 'twice'?"

"Before you crashed… I was trying to work up the sack to kill myself."

"Because of the situation with this Copeland guy?"

"That… and Ronnie leaving me. You know."

Tom watched wet snowflakes angle in at the windscreen for a few moments, measuring his reply. Then he said, "To be honest, Dale, she doesn't sound like your type. Frankly, neither does the lifestyle."

Dale said, "Correct on both counts, I guess. But at the time I felt like I had no other option. The last thing Ronnie said to me was I should use the gun on myself, save Ed the trouble. It felt like the only honest thing she'd ever said to me. It felt like the truth. I actually had the gun in my hand before you came through the wall. But I couldn't do it." What he said next was almost a whisper: "Fear. The fucking fear."

Dale got his wallet out of his jacket pocket, fished out a small snapshot and handed it Tom. Tom switched on the overhead to have a look.

It was a faded black-and-white of a gorgeous woman in her mid-twenties, her pageboy doo and flower-print dress dating the shot to the late sixties, her smile and girlish demeanour hinting at a playful sensuality.

Handing it back, Tom said, "She's beautiful. Who is she?"

"My mom."

Tom waited until Dale had replaced the photo in his wallet, then switched off the overhead.

"She split from my dad when I was twelve. He was a criminal and so was she. It's a family thing, like if your dad was a pilot."

"He was."

"Instead of getting a job to pay the bills, Mom ran cons. She was good at it, too. Used Ed in some of them, till I got old enough. But I never really acquired the knack. I screwed up a lot. The last time, when I was nine, I screwed up and got her arrested. She got cancer in jail and six months later she weighed eighty pounds. A month after that she was dead. Ed's never said as much, but I know he blames me."

"So this lifestyle, it's ..."

"Penance."

In that moment it occurred to Tom that Dale might be conning him right now...but he didn't think so. Which was the hallmark of a great con, was it not? The whole object of a con, *any* con, was to convince its intended victim to *believe*, no matter how outrageous the premise and no matter what the cost. Christ, it was like pondering time travel. It was a line of thinking that could just go round and round. In the end, what convinced him to believe Dale's story—for the time being, at least—was a simple question: What did the man have to gain by lying? No matter which way Tom looked at it, he couldn't come up with an answer that made any sense.

"Watching her wither away like that," Dale said, almost to himself now, "in a prison hospital bed, that's when the fear really took root. And it's just never gone away. What happened today made me realize it. It's why I've always wanted to be more like my brother...fuck that: it's why I've always wanted to *be* my brother. Because Ed's not afraid of anything. Never has been. And if he wants something, he just takes it. He's looked after me ever since." Straightening in his seat, Dale said, "But here's the thing. All of that bullshit vanished when I was trapped under-water. All I wanted then was to live."

He looked at Tom now, as if to gauge his response. What he saw must have pleased him because he said, "I'm gonna let you in on a little secret. I've never told this to anyone, not even my mother…but you know what I've wanted almost all my life? More than anything?"

Tom thought: *The bastard is charming, I have to give him that.* But he said, "Tell me."

"You laugh, I'll—"

"*Tell* me."

"My own pizza joint."

Tom smiled, saying, "Dale's Deep Dish?"

"My uncle Frank owned one for years and I always loved it there. Worked a bunch of summers for him until Ed started ragging me for smelling like anchovies and working for minimum wage. I'm telling you this because I want you to know how grateful I am to you for saving my ass back there."

Tom thought that if anything about all of this was genuine, it was the man's intense discomfort in this moment. Grinning, he said, "That was hard for you, wasn't it."

"Like pissing a peach pit."

"In that case, you're welcome." Tom released a sigh of his own now, his mind turning again to the prospect of getting home. He said, "Man, this has been bar none the strangest day of my life."

Cheered, Dale said, "Just another day at the office. I would *kill* for a big greasy Wendy's burger right now."

"Forget that. My wife's lasagna. And a huge vat of Pepsi with crushed ice."

"Mountain Dew."

"I stand corrected." Tom checked the dash clock: 10:03 p.m. "God, she must be frantic."

"Your wife?"

"Yeah. Mandy. You know what my last thought was before I hit that cottage? It wasn't fear. It was regret. That I'd never see my family again. Never meet my new son."

But Dale's attention had drifted. "Dale's Deep Dish," he said. "I like it. Three Ds. Needs a gimmick, though. Maybe give away free 3D glasses…"

Tom said, "Sounds like a great—" and Dale said, "*Holy fuck*," and sat ramrod straight in his seat, pointing out his side window into the woods. "There's a naked guy out there running through the trees."

Not even bothering to check, Tom said, "You're still high, aren't you," and Dale gave him an indignant 'Who me ?' look. Tom said, "I saw the syringes."

Smirking, Dale said, "Maybe a little."

"Morphine?"

"Heroin," Dale said, looking over his shoulder into the pursuing darkness. "But I could have sworn…"

"You're a piece of work," Tom said, and Dale said, "That's what my brother always says."

They laughed a little then, but it had a strained quality now. Both men were exhausted.

"We still have a long way to go," Tom said, not wanting to talk anymore, numbly perplexed at how he'd ended up chauffeuring a heroin addict out of the back country in a stolen vehicle, still trying to wrap his head around the fact that he'd killed a man and would somehow have to keep the truth of that to himself for the rest of his days. He said, "Maybe you should try and sleep it off."

His attention obviously wandering again, Dale said, "You mind if I turn the radio on?" and Tom nodded his assent. "There might be something about your plane crash. Or the murders."

As it turned out, there was nothing about either.

30

RONNIE DIDN'T HAVE LONG TO WAIT. Sumit's Mercedes rolled
to a stop at the intersection less than twenty minutes into her
stake-out, signaling a right hand turn onto the highway, its tinted
windows making it impossible for her to see inside.

And she realized then that she'd been hoping to see Dale in
there, alive and well in the back seat, when she knew without
the faintest trace of a doubt there was no way these guys were
going to bring him home in one piece.

Fucking Dale, she thought. *And fuck me for giving a shit.*

She didn't have a plan, but that didn't concern her. If she
was going to get her shit back from these two, it was going to
be more about opportunity and thinking on her feet. Whatever
it was, it would have to be bold. Toronto was a five hour drive
away, longer if the weather flared up again. Do them at a gas bar,
maybe. Or right now, when they pulled in to retrieve the Ram.
The thought made her snicker. *Won't get far in that fucking thing.*

But they made the turn without pulling in, and Ronnie's
hackles went up. Ed loved that drafty fucking truck.

She waited almost a minute, then rolled onto the highway
in pursuit.

31

SANJ TUCKED HIS BACKUP PIECE into the waistband of his pants and zipped up his overcoat. The rescue chopper was on the ice now and he didn't want the crew coming into the cottage. He slipped Sumit's lighter into his pants pocket and hurried out the front door, tucking his chin down against the wind as he plodded through the snow to the lake-facing side of the building.

Two SAR techs in bright orange flight suits were already making their way up the embankment from the chopper, one of them playing the moon-white beam of a flashlight over the wreckage of the Cessna.

Feigning a limp, Sanj moved toward them now, waving as they spotted him and the flash beam shifted to strike him in the face.

"Thank God," he said, shading his eyes as the men hastened to close the distance. "I thought I was going to freeze to death up here."

The techs had white name tags sewn onto the breast pockets of their flight suits: P. Jones and T. Carter. Jones was a little guy, mid twenties, maybe; but Carter, clearly the more experienced of the two, was big and looked like he could handle himself. Sanj decided to concentrate on Carter, who took the lead right away.

"Tom Stokes?" Carter said, looking skeptical.

Sanj said, "That's me," and it occurred to him then that he mustn't look like much of a bush pilot standing out here in his suit and thousand dollar overcoat; but if we was going to hitch a ride out of here, he needed to convince these two, at least until he was on the aircraft.

Carter said, "Are you hurt? There's blood on your neck."

"Just a little ding on the back of the head," Sanj said. "I got lucky."

Both men were looking up at the wreckage now, the little guy saying, "Are there any others?"

"All alone," Sanj said. "Glad to see you boys."

Carter gave Jones a nod and the man started moving toward the cottage. Sanj stumbled into him and Jones grabbed his arm, Carter closing in on the opposite side to do the same.

"Actually," Sanj said, "I'm feeling quite dizzy all of a sudden."

"You might be going into shock," Carter said. "Let's get you aboard."

Arms slung over the shoulders of his rescuers, Sanj let them lead him to the waiting chopper. The rotors were still spinning and Sanj was temporarily blinded by a tempest of ice pellets and snow.

Then he was on board, cuffing meltwater from his eyes while performing a quick assessment of his new environment: two pilots, a flight engineer in the rear of the aircraft and the two SAR guys. Crowd control might be an issue. He'd have to choose his moment.

But things were already beginning to unravel, Carter telling the Jones kid to run back up to the cottage and evaluate the scene, explaining to the rookie as he led Sanj to the treatment area that in spite of a victim's assurances, it was important for the team to verify for themselves the presence or absence of further casualties, Carter saying that, particularly where head injuries were concerned, the on-site testimony of the victim might be erroneous or distorted by trauma or shock.

To further complicate matters, the pilot was talking on the radio now, mumbling shit Sanj couldn't hear and eyeballing him like he had two heads.

The Jones kid was already halfway up the incline to the cottage.

Carter said, "Let's get your coat off and get you up on the stretcher here," and Sanj shot him in the knee. Carter went down hard and the flight engineer got to his feet. Sanj aimed the gun at him, saw that Jones had failed to hear the small calibre report over the chop of the rotors and shot the engineer in the left shoulder, shifting his aim to the cockpit as the engineer hit the deck.

"Hands, gentlemen," Sanj said, stepping over Carter—on his back now, clutching his ruined knee—and the men raised their hands.

"What's this about?" the pilot said.

"It's about a new flight plan," Sanj said and handed him the documents he'd retrieved from the Cessna. "Now let's get this fucker airborne, shall we?"

The copilot said, "What about Jones?" and Sanj said, "I'd rate his chances higher out there. Now I need your wallets, boys. All of them."

* * *

Once they were in the air, Sanj secured Carter to his seat with stout plastic cable-ties he kept in his coat for the purpose; the man's kneecap was shattered but the bleeding wasn't brisk enough to worry about him dying any time soon. Sanj hadn't decided yet what he was going to do with these guys, but wanted to keep them functional for the time being, in case he needed them.

Next he marched the engineer at gunpoint to the cockpit and held the gun to his temple, saying to the pilot, "Disable the radio or this man dies."

The pilot switched the radio off.

Sanj said, "I said disable it," and fired a round into the radio.

The pilot said, "*Hey*. Be careful with that thing or you'll kill us all."

"Consider that the next time I tell you to do something," Sanj said. "Does this aircraft have a GPS tracking system?"

"ELT," the pilot said. "Same principle."

"Where is it?"

"In the back."

To the copilot Sanj said, "You can fly this bird on your own, am I right?"

"Yes."

Sanj gripped the flight engineer's wounded shoulder and turned the man to face him. "Go get the ELT and make it quick," he said. "Fuck around and I'll put a bullet in your Captain's skull."

He turned next to Carter. "Now, let's see about getting this head wound of mine closed."

32

STIRRING AS IF FROM A TRANCE, Mandy shifted in her chair, her hand going to the small of her back where a nasty kink had taken up residence. She leaned away from the pain, stretching to the limit her massive belly would allow, and gradually the discomfort subsided.

The snow was still coming down out there, but that fierce wind had tapered off, only the occasional gust now, twisting the dry flakes into ghostly eddies in the deck light.

She picked up her untouched coffee and, ignoring the oily little slick that had formed on its surface, took a tentative sip. *Cold.* She shivered and set the cup back in its saucer.

The radio emitted only static, as it had without interruption in the nearly four hours since her conversation with Captain Tremblay at Search and Rescue. The Captain had done his best to reassure her, smoothly reciting the expected platitudes, but Mandy could hear the resignation in his voice, in the carefully modulated tone intended to brace her in spite of his words. She was an experienced pilot herself; she understood the odds. But Tremblay didn't know her husband. He'd come through much worse than this with a smile on his face and a great story to tell.

Every fibre of her being told her that Tom was fine, probably sharing a beer right now with an ice fisherman in a cozy hut somewhere, sitting it out like she'd told him to. If she had any sense she'd go to bed, let him wake her in the morning with a bristly kiss—

Mandy stiffened in her chair, her ears perking up.

A helicopter...?

She rose stiffly and rounded the desk to the big window, gathering her robe around her in the night-time chill of the office. Once in a blue moon a domestic air ambulance flew over the lake on its way to the hospital in Sudbury, forty kilometres away, but usually at altitude and rarely in this kind of weather. This chopper was heavier, almost military looking. And it was getting ready to land.

The aircraft hovered briefly at the edge of her line of site, five hundred metres away at the mouth of the bay, then angled off behind a line of conifers, moving farther up the lake.

Mandy settled back in her chair and used the landline to dial the direct number Captain Tremblay had given her.

33

SANJ STOOD BEHIND THE PILOT with his gun pressed to the man's neck as the chopper touched down on the ice. They'd overflown Stokes Aviation on the way in, giving him a few seconds to get the lay of the land, then chosen a more remote spot further up the lake to set down.

He'd already gagged and cable-tied Carter and the engineer to a metal handrail in the rear of the aircraft, and as the chopper powered down he did the same to the pilots, giving them one of the speeches he reserved for this final act in the proceedings, the kind that used to amuse the shit out of Sumit, because no matter what he told any of the poor bastards unfortunate enough to be hearing it, the outcome was always the same.

But this time he wasn't so sure. Without his brother here, it just didn't feel right. And as much as he'd been doing his best to block out the horror of what had happened to the kid, he could feel some vital part of himself withering inside.

"If I was going to do this right," he told them, "I'd waste every last one of you and set this noisy fucker on fire. But to be honest, I admire the work you do. Back home in India my father was a chest surgeon, and he would rise furious from the ashes if he knew of the savage path his sons had chosen. So you have him to thank for your lives. Remember that. My only hope is that he will forgive my brother Sumit when they meet before Ganesh." He could see the men had no idea what he was talking about, but he was beyond caring; it just needed to be said. "I am the one who seduced him into this life of evil. I am the one who should be dead."

He stared into the eyes of each of the crew members in turn, holding their gaze without blinking until each of them looked away. Then he said: "But if even one of you causes me grief of any kind, now or in the future…" He drew the men's wallets from an inside coat pocket. "I know where you live. And even from prison, I can reach you."

Pulling his task into focus again, Sanj unloaded the rest of the clip into the chopper's control panel, sending sparks and shrapnel flying everywhere, filling the cockpit with smoke. Then he replaced the spent clip with a fresh one and got out of the helicopter.

The wind had scoured the bulk of the snow from the lake, making it easier to walk. Ten minutes tops, he'd be there.

34

"HONESTLY, MRS. STOKES," Captain Tremblay said, his voice strained sounding in the receiver, "I can't tell you if it's our bird or not. The last report we got from our team came in about forty minutes ago. At that time they had just brought your husband on board—"

"They'd just what?" Mandy said. "They found him? Is he all right?"

"Yes, I'm sorry, yes, he's fine. I—"

Mandy said, "Forty minutes you've known this?" her relief shading abruptly to irritation with this man who should have known better. "Forty minutes and it didn't occur to you to let me know? Do you have any idea what I've been going through here, Captain Tremblay?"

"You're right. Of course you're right, Mrs. Stokes, and I do apologize. But to be frank, I didn't want to worry you any more than you already are."

"What do you mean?"

"Well, we're still not sure what's going on, but a few minutes after the Griffon reported in, it went dark. Since then we've been working under the assumption they went down in the storm.

The strange thing is, we can't even pick up their ELT. It's as if they vanished."

Mandy rubbed absently at her tummy below the navel, the muscles there achy and tense. The incessant nausea was having its way with her again.

She said, "Well, I'm no expert, Captain, but the helicopter that flew past here just a few minutes ago sure looked military. And why else would there be a chopper out here at night in this kind of weather, buzzing our lake?"

"I honestly don't know what to tell you, Mrs. Stokes. All I can suggest is that you sit tight and see what happens. If it's our aircraft and your husband is on it, you should know soon enough. Dropping him off at home would be highly irregular, however. We do have protocols."

Mandy heard the front door open, then a jingle of keys. Smiling, she said, "Oh, he just came in. Can you hold?" But there was only silence over the receiver now, not even that faint hum of live wires. She said, "Captain Tremblay? Hello?"

Assuming the storm had taken out the lines, Mandy hung up and rushed toward the office door. An East Indian man in an expensive overcoat was waiting for her there, the gun in his hand aimed casually at her chest, and Mandy let out a terrified squeal.

"You must be Mandy," the man said. "You may call me Sanj." His eyes, dark and remote, scanned the room behind her with that same casual air, then settled on her belly. "Oh, my," he said. "When are you due?"

Heart racing, Mandy sagged against the door jam, hands clutching the bulge of her abdomen. Breathless, she said, "Who are you? What do you want?"

"My name is Sanj, as I just said. You really must pay attention, Mrs. Stokes. Are we clear on that much, at least?"

Mandy nodded, bile rising in her throat.

"Your husband and his new friend have something that belongs to an associate of mine. I'm here to get it back."

"What are you talking about? My husband is missing. He…"

"That's the last thing he is, Mrs. Stokes," Sanj said, waving the gun at her. "Now sit."

On the verge of a faint, Mandy retraced her steps to the desk, feeling his flat gaze on her back as she pulled out the chair and eased herself into it. She had no idea what was going on. She watched in silence as he drew the curtains on all the windows, praying that Steve wouldn't make a peep in his bed upstairs. His room was directly overhead.

Now the man sat on the edge of the desk, right next to her, the gun resting on his thigh, its muzzle aimed at her belly.

In her terror she thought, *Sharp dressed man*, and brought a hand up to stifle a scream or maybe a bray of deranged laughter. She had to get her bearings here. Keep it together. Find out what this guy wanted and give it to him so he'd leave before—

He said, "Do you have a cell phone?"

"Yes."

"May I have it, please?"

Mandy grabbed her purse off the desk and started to open it.

"Just…hand it to me," Sanj said, making a move toward her with the gun.

Mandy handed him the purse and Sanj took her cell phone out of it. He rummaged around in the purse for a moment, then handed it back to her. Mandy took it and bunched it into her lap, clutching it as she might a buoy in a churning sea.

Sanj pocketed the cell phone, then placed the photograph

he'd taken from the Cessna on the desk in front of her. Mandy remembered signing it and giving it to Tom for good luck.

"Now," Sanj said, "where's the kid?"

35

ONLY TWENTY-FIVE MINUTES FROM THE CITY NOW and they were marooned behind a lumbering snow plow, the twisting glare of its warning lights and the ceaseless, shifting snow plumes from the blade making any chance of passing the thing an impossibility.

As Tom had expected, the smoother ride on the highway had lulled Dale into a nod, and for the past half-hour the guy had been twitching, mumbling and drooling onto his jacket collar.

Tom was hungry now, uncomfortably so, and the ache in his head had taken up the beat of his heart, each throb cranking his anxiety to a tighter setting. He kept thinking of Mandy, helpless and alone at home—surely she'd gotten Steve off to bed by now—the poor girl worried sick about him. He should have waited for the rescue chopper and to hell with this junkie dipshit, whatever weight of sympathy he'd felt for the guy earlier long since shed. In all likelihood he'd be airborne on a rescue chopper by now, talking to his wife on the radio, telling her he'd be home in a few hours to collect on that special birthday gift she'd hinted at...

"Some fucking birthday," Tom said.

Stirring, Dale said, "It's your birthday?"

"Yeah. My son and I both."

"Hey, how cool is that?" Dale said, rubbing the sleep from his eyes.

"I wish to hell I could call home, let them know I'm all right. We should've checked those guys for cell phones."

"Might be one in the vehicle someplace," Dale said, popping open the glove box.

Tom glanced over at the lighted compartment, but saw only a thin sheath of maps and what looked like a vehicle owner's manual.

"I'll have a look back here," Dale said, taking off his seat belt and leaning into the back seat. Tom heard him say, "Holy fuck," then watched him settle back into the passenger seat with a gym bag and briefcase in tow.

"What's that?"

Dale said, "Holy *fuck*," and set the briefcase on his lap, topside up. "Those crazy fuckers must have caught up with Ronnie…poor bitch."

"What is it?"

Dale opened the briefcase and turned it to face Tom, giving him a full view of the neat stacks of fifties and hundreds, new bills gleaming in the wash of the snow plow's psychedelic light show.

Wide-eyed, Tom said, "God damn."

"Yeah. Two hundred and fifty κ worth of God damn."

Dale closed the briefcase and hauled the gym bag up on top of it, giving it an affectionate pat. "And another two-fifty in product."

"Product?"

"Uncut heroin."

Tom hit the brakes, swerved to a stop at the side of the road
and powered open Dale's window. "Toss that shit out," he said,
"*right now*, or take it and get the hell out."

Dale gave him a puzzled look. "Whoa, Tom, hold on a
minute. Don't you see? This is my ticket *out* of this mess. All I've
gotta do now is hand this shit back to Ed and with any luck he
can square it with Copeland. He already knows it was Ronnie,
but the way things stood, he had no choice. He *had* to send his
goons after me. It was his ass or mine."

"Meanwhile I'm driving around with enough heroin and
drug money to land me in prison for the rest of my life."

"Just get me as far as the city," Dale said, "wherever you stop
to call your wife. After that, you never have to see me again.
Please, man."

"Jesus Christ."

Ignoring every rational instinct in his body, Tom angled the
Mercedes back onto the highway. A few minutes later they were
stuck in the snow plow's wake again, its snailing pace stretching Tom's patience to its fraying limits. He knew there was a gas
station/convenience store along here somewhere, an old Mom
& Pop outfit that would have a phone he could use, but he feared
the owners might have closed up early because of the weather.

That fear was allayed when they rounded a bend and Tom
saw the brightly lit store and a half dozen vehicles idling in the
lot, the neon OPEN sign sizzling red in the window.

Dale said, "Payphone."

"I see it," Tom said, and pulled into the lot, parking alongside
the open-air booth at the corner of the building. He switched
off the engine and got out with the keys in his hand. Dale got
out, too, bringing the briefcase and gym bag with him, stamping
his feet against the cold while Tom dug in his pocket for change.

"Why'd you bring that shit out here?" Tom said, finding some coins.

"It's my life."

Tom considered saying, *'Do you have any idea how pathetic that sounds?'* but thought better of it. He was seconds away from hearing Mandy's voice and could already feel himself grinning.

* * *

Trailing by fifty yards, Ronnie saw the Mercedes hang a left at a convenience store and she slowed, welcoming the adrenalin surge as she rolled up on the entrance to the parking lot, vivid scenarios playing out in her mind now, how she'd settle the score with those Indian fucks, ambush them as they came out of the store, maybe, or pull Sumit's trick and wait for them in the Mercedes, put a bullet in each of their swelled heads, take her shit back and hit the road before anyone knew the difference.

The place was surprisingly busy, given the weather and the late hour, but she knew that could work in her favour. Gunfire meant panic and confusion, witnesses coming up with conflicting accounts in the aftermath, throwing the cops off the scent. She'd have to keep an eye out for security cameras, but doubted that a place like this even bothered.

The Mercedes was parked parallel to the right hand corner of the building, the headlights off, no exhaust coming from the tailpipe, but there was no sign of Sumit or Sanj. There was no way they could have gotten into the store in the few seconds it had taken her to catch up, so they must still be in the vehicle. Probably waiting for the two white guys at the payphone to—

"What the fuck?"

It was Dale. Dale with the dope and the money, stamping his feet like the pussy he was. How in the fuck did *he* get here?

And who was the guy with him, dropping coins into the phone over there and grinning like an idiot? One of Copeland's men?

And why weren't Ed's monkeys getting out of the suv? *Could* they have made it into the store that quickly? It didn't seem likely; the entrance was at least thirty feet from the vehicle.

Ronnie parked the Chevy at the other end of the long building, between a van and another pickup the owner had backed in, its low bed giving her an unobstructed view of the phone booth and the entrance to the store. None of these guys knew what she was driving, so the element of surprise was still hers.

But she couldn't figure out what was going on and the confusion was killing her will to act. Were Sumit and Sanj actually taking Dale back to his brother in one piece? That didn't sound like Ed. And even if they were, why were they letting him anywhere near Copeland's property?

Where *were* those two bastards?

She decided to sit tight and see what happened.

* * *

The phone looked pretty beat up, but when Tom dropped in a few coins he got a dial tone. He punched in his home number and got a recorded message telling him the number he had dialed was no longer in service, the message followed by a repetitive beeping sound.

He said to Dale, "Storm must have taken out the lines," hung up and scooped his change out of the coin return. "I'll try her cell." This time it rang and Tom flashed a big smile at Dale; he couldn't help himself.

But the smile collapsed when he heard a man's voice on the other end of the line: "Tom? Is that you?"

Tom said, "Who is this?" But he knew; the accent was

unmistakable. As if in a wind tunnel he heard Dale say, "Tom, what is it?" but he had to brace himself against the booth to prevent his legs from folding underneath him, and when he tried to answer all that came out was a dry croak.

The voice on the phone said, "You don't remember me, Tom? I certainly remember you. That is one hell of a swing you got there, Mr. Mantle."

Feeling the fury rise in him now, Tom said, "It's Sanj, am I right? Listen, Sanj, or whoever the *fuck* you are, if you hurt my family…" but the bluster in him shrank as the reality of the situation rushed in on him. He was miles from home, utterly helpless.

He heard Sanj say, "My business is not with you, Mr. Stokes," and in the beat of silence that followed Tom clung to a thin reed of hope.

He glanced at Dale and realized what that brief silence was for: Sanj was giving his scrambled brain time to arrive at the obvious.

Now Sanj was speaking again, saying, "Do I need to explain the rules?" and Tom said, "No."

Tom looked squarely at Dale now, a cold understanding arcing the distance between them. For a heartbeat it looked as if Dale was ready to drop his cargo and bolt, but Tom's coiled posture told him there would be little point; Tom would run him down and stomp him into submission.

He snugged the receiver to his ear and waited.

* * *

Sanj was sitting on the edge of Steve's bed with Mandy's cell phone pressed to his ear, his chill gaze fixed on the boy's sleeping face.

Mandy stood hunched next to the bed, her own gaze locked on this deranged intruder still in his overcoat, Mandy ready to pounce on him and gouge those black eyes out of his skull should he betray even the slightest intention of harming her boy.

In the tense silence of the room she could hear Tom's voice over the cell, just his words not their tenor.

At least he was still alive.

And as long as he was alive Mandy knew that he would do everything in his power to get them out of this, whatever this was.

Now Sanj said, "Do I have to explain the rules?" and she heard Tom say, "No."

Sanj said, "Excellent."

And then Tom, tinny and distant: "Can I speak to my wife?"

Sanj looked up at her, his gaze measuring. "I'm not sure that would be such a good idea right now," he said, still staring, a dim amusement in his expression that Mandy wanted to claw off his face. "She might be a little... strident. And we don't want to wake the boy." He stroked Steve's hair, making him stir. "He's sleeping soundly with his teddy, the one with the button eyes. Do you believe me?"

* * *

Shivering, tears freezing to his face, Tom stared at the convenience store wall and said, "Yes," into the phone.

"All right, then," he heard Sanj say. "One more thing."

"Yes?"

"Bring the idiot with you."

The line went dead.

Tom cradled the receiver, a dozen conflicting thoughts and impulses having their way with him as he huddled there unmoving, fists clenched into bludgeons. He thought, *Rules? What rules? There are no rules, you crazy motherfucker.*

He glanced at Dale, hunched pale and trembling in the wind, understanding scribbled all over his stricken face, and wanted to kill him right where he stood, really *kill* him, snatch that briefcase out of his hand and beat him to death with it.

Unable to look at the man any longer, Tom dropped his gaze and thought of calling the cops, have them send in a s.w.a.t. team, go in there hard and blow that sick bastard straight to hell. How dare he break into their *house*—

Dale's hand on his shoulder first startled then defused him, and in this mad, reeling moment he was glad he wasn't alone.

"He's got my wife and son," Tom said. "He was *in* my son's bedroom." And before Dale could respond, Tom knew what had to be done. He said, "Get in the truck."

Hesitating, Dale held the money and the drugs out to him. "Here," he said, "take this and go. It's what he's after, anyway. If I go with you, I'm a dead man."

"If you *don't* go with me, my family is dead. Now get in the truck."

"He's going to kill us all anyway. You know that, don't you?"

"That's a chance we'll have to take."

But Dale still didn't move, and in this frozen tableau Tom felt himself on the verge of just punching the guy, hitting him so hard in that dim, selfish face he wouldn't wake up until that psycho Sanj had taken him in trade for Mandy and Steve.

Raising his fist, he said, "This is your bullshit, Dale, you have to deal with it. Now get in the truck before I beat you unconscious and drag you in there myself."

Another tense moment, then Dale complied. And as Tom opened the passenger door for him, he thought he saw some real conflict in the man's eyes, the old Dale ready to drop every-thing and run, a newer version realizing that maybe it was time to man up. Or maybe he was just kidding himself.

Then Dale was belting himself in and Tom swung the door shut and ran around the hood to the driver's side. As he climbed in and slotted the key in the ignition, he saw Dale reach into the open gym bag at his feet, pull out one of the guns he'd taken off the brothers and aim it right at his face.

Tom raised his hands in the air.

In a trembling voice, Dale said, "Don't ever threaten me again."

Tom nodded, waiting.

Then Dale let the gun spin on his finger and handed it to Tom, butt first. "You'll probably be needing this," he said.

Tom took the gun, tucked it under his seat and started the engine. Beside him, Dale dug the other gun out of the bag and stuck it into his coat pocket.

As Tom accelerated across the lot, Dale said, "This is so fucked. How did that savage prick find your place? And how did he get there so fast?"

"My pilot's license," Tom said. "I keep it on the visor." He looked at Dale as the rest of it dawned on him. "The rescue heli-copter. Jesus Christ, he hijacked the rescue chopper."

"Those poor buggers," Dale said, raising his reddened hands to the warm breath of a dash vent. "How much farther?"

"Little under an hour if the weather holds," Tom said, pausing at the verge to let a Greyhound barrel past. "Fifteen minutes to the city, forty more to the house."

Numb, Tom guided the GL onto the highway, the pickup truck pulling out behind him barely registering in his frantic mind.

36

BACK IN THE OFFICE SANJ sat the woman at her desk, draped his coat over the back of the couch and sat in the matching arm chair to call Ed. The part of him that should have been grieving his brother's death tugged at him again, but for the most part his primary instinct was to stick to the plan. Business as usual. It would be what Sumit would expect of him. He could concern himself with his brother later.

His reaction to losing his parents had been essentially the same—contrasting sharply with Sumit's open glee in anticipation of the sizeable inheritance they were about to share—but, on the surface at least, Sanj attributed his attenuated emotions to simple professionalism. The ability to compartmentalize one's emotions was essential to this kind of work. You were given a task and paid extremely well for carrying it out. You had to think on your feet and remove obstacles as they appeared, whatever those obstacles might be, and without hesitation.

When the topic came up between him and his brother, Sumit was generally more blunt in his assessment. "We're sociopaths, bro. All predators are. It only makes sense. It keeps things tidy and neat. Fillet a motherfucker with a blade and an hour later you're sipping cocktails and bird-dogging bitches without a care in the world. Unless the fucker got blood on your boots." And my, how he would laugh...

Sanj noticed the woman staring at him, grimacing and holding her belly, and averted his eyes to punch in Ed's number on the cell. He hated this homey fucking place and wanted only to get this over with. The only good thing so far was that the kid had remained asleep in his bed. He hadn't yet made up his mind about what to do with these two, and having to put up with a bawling kid would almost certainly hasten a decision.

* * *

Mandy ground her teeth against a cramp that felt like a hot poker thrust in through her lower back and out through her vagina. *Dear God*, she thought, *please... not now.*

She held her breath and gradually the pain subsided. Sweat beaded her brow in spite of the chill in the office. She felt like she had to go to the bathroom.

Instead, she watched Sanj, listening as he explained the situation to someone named Ed, his boss, Mandy assumed, given his tone. Tom had crashed the Cessna into a cottage and had somehow gotten mixed up with this other guy, Dale. Sanj and someone else had intercepted a woman named Ronnie and retrieved the 'package', but Dale and Tom had killed the someone and gotten away? Was that what he just said? None of it made any sense.

She prayed Steve would not wake up.

Please, baby. Please, whatever you do, don't come down here...

* * *

Speaking into the phone, Sanj said, "They're on their way here now," and heard Ed say, "Good. See if you can't get it right this time. And Sanj…"

"Yes, Ed?"

"I'm sorry about your brother."

"Thank you."

"I'll take care of the mess at the cottage, soon as we hang up. I know some people up there; they'll handle it. No trace."

"Okay, Ed."

"All right. Call me when it's done. I've got to square this with Copeland by mid-afternoon tomorrow. I need that shit back here a-sap. Morning at the latest."

Sanj said, "Consider it done," but Ed had already hung up.

He stood, set the cell phone on the hardwood floor and crushed it under his boot heel. In the same instant the woman screamed at the top of her lungs and a great gush of fluid splashed onto the floor beneath her, soaking her night dress and legs.

Sanj said, "What the fuck is that?"

But Mandy only groaned, her face a taut sketch of agony.

Rubbing sleep from his eyes, the kid came padding into the room now, his teddy dangling from one hand.

"Mommy?"

37

BY THE TIME THEY REACHED ELM STREET, the main drag through downtown Sudbury, the blizzard had all but stopped, just a few lazy flakes now, drifting from a low sky tinted orange by the city Halogens.

Tom braked for a red light at the corner of Elm and Durham and a cop car pulled up next to him in the left hand lane. Tom fixed his gaze on the road ahead and said, "Oh, shit," repeating it again and again through clenched teeth.

"Relax, man," Dale said. "No reason for them to be interested in us."

"The psychos that own this vehicle, you think you can say that? They're probably running the plates right now."

"On a night like this," Dale said, "that's unlikely in the extreme." He pointed up the street to the Tim Horton's at the next intersection. "See that Timmy's up there?"

Tom nodded, both fists clamped on the steering wheel.

"Ten to one that's where they're headed. Just be cool. Don't give them a reason to be suspicious. A good cop is like a dog… he can smell fear."

"Your brother tell you that?"

"Yeah."

Tom froze his gaze front and centre for as long as he could, quietly cursing the needlessly long red light at this time of night...but he couldn't help himself.

He looked out his side window and saw the cop in the shotgun seat staring up at him. His instinct was to look away, but he smiled and nodded, thinking, *Jesus, what the hell is wrong with me?*

The cop held his gaze for a long beat, not responding, then turned to face the road.

Now the light changed and the cruiser pulled away.

Tom just sat there, idling.

Dale said, "It's green."

Then the car behind them honked, breaking the spell, and Tom eased ahead, letting the cruiser gain some distance on them. Exhaling, he said, "How well do you know this guy?"

"Sanj? The man's crazy as a shithouse rat, that much I do know. What I didn't know is that he and that other greaser were brothers. They're always with Ed, as in *always*, but before tonight neither one of them even said boo to me. They just sit there, looking dense. I think that's part of why they're so good at what they do. You just don't expect it...and then *boom*, you're dead. Call me a racist, but who expects a parking lot attendant to pull a gun on them?"

"I get the picture."

"Sorry, man. I'm a touch A.D.D. And I'm scared shitless."

"Most of those parking lot attendants you're talking about have degrees in physics or engineering."

"I know. They're not stupid."

"What I'm getting at is, on the phone he made it clear that we should come alone...but should I involve the police anyway?"

As they tracked through the next intersection, watching the cruiser pull into the Tim Horton's drive thru, Dale said, "Truthfully? The last thing I want is to have to face that fucker again. So yeah, my first impulse is to say 'Absolutely. Hell, yeah, call the cops, let them handle it.' But he'll see them coming, Tom. And he'll waste your family. He'll do that without even blinking and then he'll take down as many cops as he can before they stop him. I have no idea what makes people like him tick or how they find their way to guys like my brother...but I've seen what they're capable of and it scares the hell out of me."

"He doesn't look like much."

"You know what they say about looks. I noticed a weird tattoo on his wrist a couple years back and did a little research on the Internet. It took some doing, but it turns out it's an Indian Special Forces tat, the insiders' insignia of the nastiest branch of the military over there, the Bharat something or other; I forget now. Mean mothers, anyway."

"Never judge a book by its cover."

"Exactly."

Tom said, "Just like you."

"What do you mean?"

"You're clearly a lot smarter than you let on."

"I read."

Tom gave him his best 'Come on, man' grin.

"It's what's expected of me," Dale said. "And it worked for Ronnie. She likes to run the show."

Tom said, "Just like your mom," but he could see that Dale had had enough.

"So what's the plan?" Dale said.

"I'm going to kill him."

38

MANDY LEANED AGAINST THE DESK, clutching the hem of her night dress, amniotic fluid dripping from the fabric into a creeping puddle at her feet. She was having another contraction and the pain was extreme, much worse than it had ever been with Steve ... and when she looked down she saw streaks of bright red blood in the mess on the floor. Not a good sign.

As the contraction heightened, Mandy closed her eyes and howled, making a sound she'd never heard before, let alone uttered. She looked up and saw Sanj standing there with his mouth hanging open, pointing the gun at her from ten feet away as if he feared something alien might slither out from between her legs and eel its way across the floor at him.

Steve had dropped his teddy and stood frozen in the doorway, staring at her with tears in his eyes. Given the circumstances, though, Mandy thought as the pain eased off, the little guy seemed incredibly self-possessed. She'd talked to him a lot about this, what it would be like when the new baby came, preparing him for the likely event that his dad might not be around when she went into labour.

But nothing could have prepared either of them for this crazed scene.

She decided to handle it as if the intruder were not there.

"Steve, honey," she said, a fresh contraction already gripping her, "your mommy's okay. This is all normal. But I need you to call the ambulance for me now, okay? Remember what we talked about?"

Nodding, Steve started toward the phone on the desk, hesitating only slightly when Mandy made a dull lowing sound, doing her best to stifle another agonized howl.

Steve picked up the receiver and Mandy said, "That's right, sweetheart. It's on speed dial. Just hit number one." She glanced at Sanj, still standing there with his mouth open, then looked again at Steve. "Go ahead, honey. Hit number one."

Steve pressed the number with a tiny finger, brought the receiver to his ear and said, "It's not working."

Quietly, Sanj said, "I cut the line."

"You what?" Mandy said, and thought she saw a trace of guilt in the man's slack expression.

"The radio, too."

"You *ass*hole. Then you have to take me to the hospital. *Right now.*"

Sanj said, "I'm afraid I can't do that," and Mandy rolled her head and uttered a banshee wail, this fresh contraction wringing her out like a giant's crushing hands. In her agony she thought, *NO. They're too close together, it's coming too fast…*

Steve padded to her side and took her hand, the poor kid tracking barefoot through the puddle of amniotic fluid that surrounded her. And watching her son do that, imagining the courage it must have taken for her tiny little man to *do* that, caused something to snap almost audibly in her brain.

And in that moment, in spite of her suffering, Mandy Stokes was just about as pissed off as she had ever been.

"Listen," she said to Sanj, "whoever the *fuck* you are. My son was born very quickly, and it feels like this one's going to do the same—"

Mandy closed her eyes and screamed again, feeling the tiny bones in her son's hand grind together in the force of her grip, feeling her insides on the verge of bursting. When she opened her eyes they were fixed on Sanj, still standing motionless ten feet away with the gun aimed at the floor now, an expression of utter bewilderment on his face.

"Wanna see something, fucker?" she said and hiked her dress up to her chin, bending to grab a quick, confirming peek before exposing herself to a now bug-eyed Sanj.

Recoiling, Sanj said, "What *is* that?"

Mandy said, "It's the baby's *head*, you idiot," before letting her soggy night dress slop back into place. "Oh…it's *coming*… you have to take me to the *hospital*…"

Steve was sobbing now and Mandy relaxed her grip on his hand, whispering to him not to worry, this was all normal, knowing that the boy knew there was exactly nothing normal about any of this but saying it anyway. She wanted to weep right along with him.

She saw Sanj glance at the door now, as if he'd like nothing better than to flee, and she wished that he would just *do* that, *prayed* that he would. Their nearest neighbour was a quarter mile up the road, Steve could dress himself and run over there, the little guy could really *run*…run over there and get them to call an ambulance…

But the crazy bastard didn't leave. Instead—surprising Mandy as another contraction wrung her out, this one bringing swarms of tiny blacks dots into the edges of her vision, signaling a black out—he holstered his weapon, threw the cushions off the sofa bed that stood next to the storage room and hauled the bed open.

Now he was marching toward her, reaching out to guide her to the bed, and Mandy shrieked, "Don't—*touch* me," and the man stopped short, raising his hands as if it were Mandy who had the gun instead of him.

Sanj said, "All right, but please, lie down over here."

Mandy tried to take a step, Steve doing his best to take some of her weight, but when she let go of the desk a fresh swirl of dizziness rose up in her, followed abruptly by another contraction—they were almost continuous now, one unbroken attempt by her body to turn her inside out—and she reached out to Sanj, saying, "Help me, you prick," and Sanj lifted her up as if she were weightless and carried her to the bed, setting her gently on her back.

Immediately Mandy came up on her elbows and wailed, bearing down involuntarily now, the sensation of impending expulsion overpowering and exquisitely painful. Sweat ran off her in rivulets and her breathing wasn't breathing at all but a series of hastily snatched gasps that made her feel like she was drowning in thin air.

Steve sat next to her in stoic silence, wrapping his hand around her wrist, holding on tight, not knowing what else to do.

Sanj scooped a couple of pillows off the floor and stuffed them between Mandy and the back of the sofa bed and Mandy braced herself against them, bringing her knees up and bearing down for all she was worth. "Oh, God, it's coming... *it's coming...* "

Sanj was standing at the foot of the bed now, and when in the frenzy of her labour Mandy peeled her dress off her belly and revealed her privates to him again, he abruptly averted his gaze.

"Please stop doing that," he said, and Mandy said, "You didn't want to take me to the hospital, motherfucker, you better get used to it, because this is happening *right now*." She cuffed a clump of sweat-soaked hair out of her eyes and said to her son, "Sorry, sweetheart, Mommy'll put a bunch of quarters in the swearing jar—" and screamed again in agony. "Call me an ambulance, you bastard. Call me a fucking AMBULANCE."

And abruptly Sanj was moving—Mandy could almost see a light going on inside his head—and she watched him dart to the desk, watched him manoeuvre the computer mouse then begin hammering at the keyboard, his body blocking her view of the screen. He clicked the mouse a few more times, then adjusted the volume of the speakers to full.

When he got out of the way Mandy could see a full-screen YouTube video starting to play, a brief flourish of funky music followed by a yellow cartoon taxi zooming onto the screen, a bold red title superimposing itself over the scene: HOW TO DELIVER A BABY IN AN EMERGENCY.

She thought, *God help me*, and growled as she bore down hard. She felt herself lapsing into a kind of exhausted trance now, the immense stress of this strange man waving a gun in her face, the dread of losing her new baby right here in the business office, the dazed silence of her terrified son, all of it receding as if in a mist, still there, still tangible, but with none of the sharp edges. Even the pain seemed far away, as if she were recalling it rather than living it.

And it was through this blessed fog that she heard a female narrator begin a voice-over in an oddly cheerful tone...

"How to deliver a baby in an emergency."

Mandy focused on the video as the scene cut to a cartoon woman lying propped on her elbows in the back seat of the taxi, the narrator crooning, *"You can see the baby's head, but there is no doctor in sight."*

The scene switched to the cab driver looking into the back seat in bug-eyed alarm, the narrator saying, *"First, calm down. Then follow these instructions."*

A title materialized over the cabbie's face: YOU WILL NEED, and beneath it a list began to appear, each item articulated by the narrator.

"You will need: Sheets. Towels or clean cloths..."

Mandy felt a new kind of pain now, an impaling agony that jerked her out of the fog and rose to a pitch beyond her ability to bear it, and for a short time everything went gloriously, mercifully black.

39

MARSHALL CRANSTON HAD BEEN OUT IN HIS YARD, waiting
for his wife's pug-nosed Pekingese to evacuate its bowels, when
the helicopter angled in for a landing on Windy Lake, not a
quarter mile from where he stood. The lake itself was shaped like
a jumbo shrimp, its eye a tiny island that supported just a single
dwelling, the converted cottage he and the old lady had been
living in since 1945, right after he got back from WWII with
a heart-shaped chunk of shrapnel in his calf and three fingers
missing from his left hand. He'd been a fighter pilot, shot down
over the South Pacific, but had never lost his love of aircraft, all
kinds of them. He had shelves of books about them, went to
every airshow he could, and every once in a while the Stokes lad
at the tail of the lake brought him up in one of his bush planes
and let him take the controls.

And even though he'd just turned eighty-nine—but felt
fifty—he was still sharp enough to realize that you didn't land a
goddam rescue chopper on the ice in this kind of weather and
then just sit there, silent and dark. There was some kind of shit
going on over there and he meant to find out what it was.

When he told his wife Myrtle he was going to hike over

146

to investigate, she insisted he take that yappy little shit factory along for the exercise. Before he left he grabbed his big Maglite flashlight, excellent for close quarters combat if it came to that, and dug his old .45 calibre service pistol out of its case and stuffed it fully loaded down the back of his pants, gangsta style.

The thing was, he was almost certain he'd heard small calibre gunfire before the chopper went dark, four distinct little *pops* in the crisp night air.

Now, here he was in his snowshoes with the damned dog straining against its rhinestone-studded leash, creeping around the tail of the helicopter with the Maglite in one hand and his pistol in the other. He could see that the big side door was wide open, snow blowing into its dark maw, but there were no signs of life.

He brought his firearm to bear and called out—"Anybody there?"—and was startled when a chorus of beseeching groans rose from inside.

"Knew it," he said and tramped to the doorway, switching the flashlight on now, its shifting beam picking out four faces in there, two of them skull-eyed and pale, the other two smiling at him through strips of duct tape. He could see that all four of them had been cable-tied by the wrists to a long metal handrail. And there was a burnt, electrical smell coming from the cockpit on thin wisps of smoke. From here it looked like someone had shot up the console.

Marshall lifted the shivering dog into the body of the aircraft then sat on the doorstep to remove his snowshoes. "Hang on, fellas," he told the crew. "I'll have you outa there in a jiffy."

40

WHEN MANDY CAME TO, there was a bed sheet draped across her bent knees and she tucked it down to see Sanj seated on a bar stool at the foot of the sofa bed with bright yellow dishwashing gloves on his hands, a breathing mask from Tom's workshop on his face and the Blood Bath butcher's apron she'd given Tom last Halloween over his clothing. The front of the apron was crisscrossed with finger smears of fake blood, which, under the circumstances, didn't seem quite so funny anymore.

Mandy was immersed in that merciful fog again and, for the moment at least, it seemed that her contractions had either slackened or ceased. Her belly was still huge, so she knew she hadn't delivered.

She was trying to summon the energy to ask Sanj where Steve was when the little guy came scuffing into the room from the main house, his fuzzy Ninja Turtles slippers on his feet now, and plunked her sewing scissors onto the collapsible tray Sanj had set up next to the bed. On the tray already were a basin of steaming water, a small stack of clean face towels and a new pair of brown shoelaces, still kinked from the package they'd come in.

She said, "How long was I out?" and Sanj said, "Not long."

Now he was saying, "Okay, Mandy, I want you to push," and Mandy giggled and told him how ridiculous he looked. Everything still seemed so surreal, the product of too much alcohol, maybe, and she was puzzled when she saw the man nod at Steve like they were old pals, then saw Steve scoot over to the computer and rest his hand on the mouse. What were they—?

Then the fog lifted like a sprung blind and the pain was back, full throttle and chromium bright, and Mandy screamed, really *howled* this time, it felt like she was being impaled from the inside, and in the seething distance she heard Sanj say, "Okay, kid, hit play," and now that tinny soundtrack was in her head again, like Fisher Price music played on a toy xylophone, and the narrator was saying, *"Once the baby's head emerges, tell the mother to stop pushing,"* and Sanj shouted, "Stop pushing! Stop pushing!" and on the tail end of a roar from bearing down so forcefully Mandy said, *"There's nothing wrong with my* HEARING*!"*

And now, into a lull, a sweet, sacred lull, came the narrator's cheery voice again...

"Step six. Gently cradle the baby's head, then prepare to catch."

In his stealthy little way, Steve appeared at her side, took her sweaty hand in his own and began gently patting it.

Over the top of the tented sheet Mandy watched Sanj avert his eyes, then reach under the sheet with both hands.

"After the shoulders slip out one at a time—"

A final, brief contraction seized her now, and as it passed Mandy let out a sigh of release. This was followed by some wet squishy sounds and the strangely gratifying sight of Sanj dry heaving into his paper mask.

"—the rest of the body will quickly follow."

There was a moment of tense silence as Sanj withdrew his arms from under the sheet, which was crimson now with real blood, *her* blood, and Mandy tucked the sheet down tight against her crotch so she could see what was going on.

Sanj stood, lifting her newborn boy into the light.

The infant was limp and blue, not breathing.

Steve said, "Is he okay?" and Mandy said, "*Do* something!"

"*Step Seven. Clear the baby's air passages by gently drying its nose and mouth with a soft clean towel.*"

Sanj grabbed a towel from the tray and began drying the baby's face with it. When that failed he flipped the infant onto its chest and began vigorously drying its back.

But the child remained flaccid.

In a panic Mandy tried to get off the bed, but she just didn't have the strength. All she could manage was a desperate chorus: "Do something…please, do something…"

"*If the baby doesn't seem to be breathing, firmly flick the bottom of its feet with a fingernail.*"

Sanj tried it, with no result.

"*If that doesn't work, blow a few gentle breaths into the baby's mouth.*"

And with an air of calm Mandy believed she would never forget, Sanj inhaled, raised up her newborn baby, sealed his lips over its nose and mouth and gently exhaled, both of them watching the infant's tiny chest inflate for the first time, then deflate as Sanj broke the seal to exhale and take a fresh breath. He did this four times in a tableau of utter, motionless silence…

Then the baby's limbs twitched, flexed…and it coughed and began to cry.

All three of them—Sanj, Mandy and Steve—whooped for joy.

"Oh, my God," Mandy said, sobbing now, her wet eyes meeting Sanj's, "thank you. Thank you."

In that moment something passed between the two adults, and for a few precious seconds it seemed to Mandy that this armed intruder who had appeared out of nowhere with cold murder in his eyes had just discovered something about himself, and it had freed him from whatever demons compelled him, and she believed that whatever had brought him here no longer mattered and after a while he would leave the way he had come, and maybe, just maybe, they would even stay in touch…

But the narrator's voice broke the spell and Sanj glanced at the computer screen, then back at Mandy before setting about the next task he was given. And in that last quick glance Mandy could see no trace of the demon banished, and knew that before this was over he would kill them all, maybe even her babies.

And instead of terror, the knowledge induced an unexpected, watchful calm.

Using the shoelaces, Sanj tied off the umbilical cord in two places then cut between them with the scissors, a few droplets of cord blood spattering the apron, the stains darker than the fake blood that was already there. A single drop caught him on the chin, and as he raised the hem of the apron to wipe it away he looked directly at Mandy and said, "Whatever happens here tonight, I will not hurt your children."

And in spite of the insanity of it all, Mandy gave him a grateful nod.

"*Step eight. Encourage the new mom to breast feed immediately.*"

Sanj bundled the newborn in a clean towel and handed him to Mandy, who put him to her breast.

"*This will help her body expel the placenta and stop her bleeding.*"

Sanj said, "Placenta?"

"*Let the placenta emerge on its own. Don't try to pull it out.*"

Sitting again, Sanj looked at the cut end of the umbilical

cord with the shoelace tied around it, following its course under the sheet into Mandy's vagina.

"Save it for the doctor, who will want to examine it later."

As Sanj lifted the sheet for a better view, Mandy gave one last exhausted push. There was a nasty wet glurping sound as she expelled the afterbirth, right under Sanj's nose. She could feel it sliding out of her like some bloated, benthic mutation.

With a rush of grim satisfaction, Many watched Sanj's eyes widen in horror.

41

TOM BROUGHT THE MERCEDES TO A STOP at the foot of the two hundred metre access road that led from the highway into Stokes Aviation. Killing the engine, he said to Dale, "We walk from here."

Leaving the heroin and the cash in the back seat, the men exited the vehicle into a calm, moonless night under a static gray sky, the storm finally spent. Facing Dale, Tom aimed an extended arm up the road, inviting him to take the lead. Whatever he believed he'd learned about Dale Knight today, he still wasn't sure he trusted the man walking behind him in the dark with a loaded gun in his possession.

Dutifully, Dale began tramping up the unplowed road toward the house, and Tom had the at once pedestrian and utterly ludicrous thought that he would have to give his plow guy shit for not having their road cleared yet. Ludicrous because after tonight, they might all be dead.

The thought sobered Tom and he reached into his pocket for the weapon Dale had given him, liking its heft, its cold assurance in his bare hand. He pulled back the slide to chamber a round. Without breaking stride in front of him, Dale said, "Be careful with that thing. If I get shot tonight, I don't want it to be by you."

Tom said, "Are you still up for this?" and Dale didn't answer.

They came around a bend in the road and Tom put a hand on Dale's shoulder, stopping him. Light from the compound was visible now through a dense stand of jack pines and Tom didn't want them getting spotted before they even reached the grounds.

The men huddled there briefly and Tom said, "I asked you if you were still up for this," and Dale said, "Fuck, no...but yes, I'm still up for this, all right?"

Tom said all right, then angled off the road into the knee-deep snow of the jack pine stand, taking the lead now, deciding to trust the terrified heroin addict with the gun in his hand who tramped into the woods behind him. When it came right down to it, what choice did he have?

They came out of the trees about twenty feet from the huge, stainless steel Quonset hut that served as a garage, repair shop and hangar, a windowless monstrosity that Mandy hated and joked could probably be seen from space.

"Okay," Tom said, "this is it. Remember the drill?"

Breathing hard beside him, Dale said, "I got it, Tom. Let's just get it done, okay?"

"All right. See you on the other side."

The men moved off in opposite directions, Dale heading past the Quonset hut to the brightly lit front of the homestead, Tom angling around back. Years ago he'd hidden a key to the rear door of the hut above its metal frame, and was gratified now to find it still there, snug in its little magnetic box. He used it to open the seldom-used door, which gave a rusty bark as he drew it open against the accumulated snow, the harsh sound fading quickly to silence in the drooping boughs of the surrounding pines.

He paused there a moment, breathing puffs of frost into the still night air, listening, fearful the sound had alerted Sanj and exposed them before they even got started…but there was nothing: no movement, no sound.

Proceeding more cautiously now, Tom used the side of his boot to clear away the banked snow, then eased the door open just wide enough to slip through.

Inside, he used a penlight to find a spare set of keys in a coffee can on his workbench, then tucked the light between his teeth, removed a single key from the ring with shivering fingers and tucked the lot of them into his pocket.

Finally, he lifted an extension ladder from its hooks and carried it out through back door.

* * *

As it had always been, Dale's first instinct was to bolt. Fuck this nonsense. Get back down to the Mercedes—*Shit, Tom has the keys*—grab the stuff and beat a trail for parts unknown. He didn't owe these people anything—it was Tom who'd crashed the party, not him—and he sure as fuck didn't want to die out here tonight. Sanj was a murdering maniac and Dale had *seen* the fury in those black eyes after he shot the man's brother, a cold, sharklike death stare that had frightened him even more than the switchblade Sanj had been about to flay him with. Truth be told, he'd come close to shitting himself right there in the tub.

He really did know a guy in Montreal who'd pay top dollar for the dope—minus the half-key he'd hold onto for personal use—and that, plus the quarter mill in cash he already had, would be more than enough to comfortably carry him for the next five years. Someplace warm and *very* far away…

In spite of himself, Dale crept up to the first window he saw and peeked inside at what looked like a living room. Dimly lit in there. Abandoned.

But fuck, if he was being honest with himself, he really *did* owe this guy. If Tom hadn't coldcocked Sanj he'd be dead right now, bled out in his uncle's bathtub. The thought of it raised a cold sweat across his scalp and for a moment, picturing it, Dale thought he might puke.

Breathing in shallow gasps, he hunched there in the shadow of the porch, hands on his knees until the feeling passed.

God *damn* it.

He'd actually taken a dozen quick steps toward the roadway when he turned, raised the gun to a ready position and started back toward the porch steps.

He thought, *Fuck this. Oh, sweet Lord Jesus, fuck this.*

Then he crept up the stairs to the patterned glass side-light and peered inside.

* * *

Tom was on the roof at the back of the house now, staring into the master bedroom through the big dormer window, barely able to make anything out in the unlit enclosure. Once his eyes adjusted, he could see that the bed was still made and Mandy's work clothes were draped across the foot rail, which probably meant she was wearing a nightie and, hopefully, a housecoat. The thought of that animal's eyes on her made his skin crawl. If he had so much as *touched* her...

But he knew this line of thinking was pointless and would only make him impulsive and vulnerable once he was face to face with the guy, and he did his best to suppress it.

He started around the east-facing side of the roof, heading for Steve's room at the front of the house. Partway there he lost his footing on the steep slope and almost went over the edge, just managing to stop himself by digging the edges of his boots into the frozen shingles.

Panting, he thought, *Shit, they* must *have heard that.*

Then Dale's voice from below, a loud whisper: "You okay up there?"

Tom peered over the edge and saw Dale staring up at him, gun aimed at the ground. Tom said, "I figured soon as I took my eyes off you, you'd make a run for it."

"Almost did," Dale said. "Thanks for the vote of confidence. And keep it down, will you?"

"Be with you in a sec. Just going to check my son's room. See anything yet?"

"Not a thing."

"Okay, wait right there."

Taking his time now, Tom crept to the front of the house and checked Steve's room, the little guy's green nightlight casting a creepy pall over everything in there. The covers on his bed were folded down, the bottom sheet wrinkled from the weight of his body, but Steve was nowhere in sight.

Tom felt his insides turn to mud. He crept back to the ladder and started down, Dale steadying his descent from the ground.

Stepping off into the snow, Tom said, "Steve's not in his bed. Why would he bring a five year old into this?"

"Insurance," Dale said.

"Well, fuck him. Did you check the office yet?" Dale shook his head and Tom said, "Okay, follow me."

He didn't want to risk exposure by using the big picture window, so he led Dale to the west-facing side of the building, coming full circle to the Quonset hut, the flank of which formed an eight-foot wide alleyway with the main structure. Near the front of the building they came to a small window in the side wall of the office, but the blind had been drawn. Mandy never drew those blinds, so it must have been Sanj.

Tom moved to the picture window next to find that the blind had been drawn on it, too. He returned to the side window and noticed a narrow space at the top where the blind was suspended from its base. He got Dale to give him a boost.

It took him a moment to orient himself, but then he saw the foot of the open sofa bed and the floor beside it. There was a blood stained sheet balled up on the floor, and the unmoving outline of two pairs of feet under a blanket on the bed, one pair adult, the other a child's.

"Oh, no…"

* * *

Setting Tom down, Dale said, "What is it?" but Tom had tears in his eyes now and appeared catatonic, swaying in a near faint.

Dale spotted a wooden skid leaning against the Quonset hut and pried it out of the snow, propped it against the office wall and scaled it to have a look for himself.

Jesus. It did not look good.

He heard Tom say, "That motherfucker," and said, "We don't know that yet, Tom," and hopped back to the ground. He said, "Did you see him?"

"No."

"Me neither. So let's just stick to the plan."

Tom nodded and handed him a key. "This is for the outside basement door; you passed it on the other side of the house."

Dale remembered.

Tom said, "You go down six steps, straight across the basement and up another twelve. That'll put you right across from the office door. He's probably watching it, so be careful. I'll be coming in through the other side of the house. If we time it right, we'll end up flanking the office door. That way, at best, he'll only be able to get the drop on one of us, no matter how clever he is."

The urge to flee welled up in Dale again, stronger this time, but Tom said, "Is your head clear?" and Dale said, "Crystal." And it was.

"All right," Tom said, and offered his hand to be shaken. Dale shook it, surprised by its gentle strength, its warmth out here in the snow.

Still holding Dale's hand, Tom said, "Thanks, Dale. And no matter what happens next, you're already twice the man your brother ever was."

Then he let go and started away and Dale stood there for a moment in the chill winter air, an absurd sting of tears in his eyes, flight the furthest thing from his mind now.

He wiped his eyes dry and got moving.

* * *

When Tom stepped into the hallway that gave onto the closed office door, a part of him still half expected Dale to have fled in the eleventh hour; but the man was already there, his back to the wall next to the office door, gun raised in a two-handed grip like a character from an action film, his expression tense, not with fear, Tom judged, but with a fierce determination.

Tom took a similar stance on the opposite side of the door and, with a confirming nod, grasped the knob and swung the door open, moving silently into the room and dropping to one knee, sweeping the area for targets. Dale stepped in behind him and remained standing, aiming over Tom's head.

No sign of Sanj.

From his current vantage a dozen feet from the sofa bed, Tom could see only its bottom third, a wider view obstructed by the big storage room he'd built the previous summer. There was still no movement on the bed, and, glancing again at that bloody sheet, Tom braced himself for the worst.

Whispering to Dale, he said, "Cover me," and rose to his full height, moving toward the bed now. He cleared the corner of the storage room, gun at the ready in case Sanj was waiting for him there, then turned his attention to his wife and son lying on their sides, facing each other as if posed, so utterly still that Tom felt certain they were dead.

Despondent, he touched Mandy's ankle through the blanket...

And Mandy opened her eyes.

Tom turned to Dale—the man still standing guard in the doorway, trying to look everywhere at once—and gave him a relieved thumbs up.

Mandy glanced at Steve, still sound asleep beside her, then looked at Tom and brought a finger to her lips. *Shh.*

Tom mouthed, "Where is he?" and Mandy pointed at the storage room.

Tom turned again to Dale and nodded at the storage room. The men aligned themselves as they had at the office door, and after a silent three count Tom swung the door open and both men aimed their guns into the starkly lit room.

Sanj was hog-tied on the floor in there, duct-taped into a fetal position with an oily rag stuffed into his mouth and a strip of tape covering his eyebrows and eyes. When he heard them come in he began to wriggle and grunt on the floor.

Dale and Tom traded stares of amazement, then Dale followed Tom back to the sofa bed. Mandy was sitting up now, the blanket tugged up to her chin.

Both men simply stared at her.

Shrugging, Mandy said, "After I delivered the placenta, he fainted."

But this served only to confuse Tom more.

With a coy smile, Mandy lowered the blanket to reveal their newborn son, soundly sleeping in her arms.

Trying to stifle a gale of laughter, Tom tucked his gun into the back of his pants and approached Mandy's side of the bed. Giggling now herself, Mandy handed him their infant son and Tom sat on the bed next to her, stunned into silence by the circumstances and the beauty of this new life, so tiny and warm in the hammock of his arms.

Tom saw the dopey grin on Dale's face and within moments all three of them were consumed by laughter, the same crazed, delighted laughter Tom had shared with Dale after the crash.

In the giddy commotion Steve sat bolt upright in bed, screwing a fist into one sleepy eye and saying, "Is it still my birthday?" and the laughter escalated to a breathless, manic pitch. Incredibly, tucked into his father's arms, the Stokes' new infant son slept through the entire thing.

* * *

Helpless on the floor in the storage room, Sanj tilted his head at the rising laughter, wondering what kind of mad asylum he'd let himself into.

42

TUCKED SAFELY INTO HIS OWN BED NOW, Steve said, "Daddy, what's going to happen to that man?"

Tom sat on the edge of the bed and snugged Steve's button-eyed Teddy into its usual sleeping spot, in the crook of Steve's left arm. "He's going to jail for a very long time."

"But he saved my baby brother," Steve said, his eyelids trying hard to close.

"Yes, he did, and we're all really grateful for that. But it doesn't mean he shouldn't be punished for all of the other bad things he's done."

Yawning hugely, Steve said," Like what?"

"Like breaking into our house and pointing a gun at you and your mommy. And that's just for starters."

But the poor kid was already fast asleep. Tom brushed the hair off the boy's smooth forehead and softly kissed him there. Then he got to his feet and, before he left, switched off the green night light; he had a feeling that after tonight, this brave little guy wouldn't be needing it anymore.

* * *

Ten minutes later Tom was sitting in the garage behind the wheel of his truck, speaking into the handset of a two-way radio to a Sudbury cop, the cop saying, "We just got a call from a guy up the lake from you says he's got the entire chopper crew in his kitchen. Two of them with non-lethal gunshot wounds. There's an ambulance on its way to them now." The cop said, "You're certain this guy is adequately restrained?"

Tom said, "He's not going anywhere."

"All right. Give us about thirty minutes."

"That's great," Tom said. "Thanks very much."

"Ten four."

When he got back to the office he saw that Dale had dragged Sanj out of the storage room and secured him upright in one of Mandy's antique kitchen chairs, enough duct tape wrapped around the man to restrain a stallion.

Mandy was sitting upright on the sofa bed now, cooing to their new son, and Dale was standing directly behind Sanj, spinning the spool of an exhausted roll of tape on his index finger.

Tom said, "I think you got him," and Dale frowned, as if he wasn't so sure.

Mandy said, "Dale gave me the condensed version. Sounds like you boys've had quite the day." Tom managed a weary grin and Mandy said, "Were you able to reach the police?" Tom nodded, telling her they'd be here in half an hour.

There were some questions he wanted to ask Sanj before the cops got here and he waved Dale over, the two of them standing in front of Sanj now.

Speaking to Dale, Tom said, "Do the honours?"

Dale said, "Gladly," grasped a corner of the tape across Sanj's eyebrows and eyes and ripped it off as brutally as he could.

Sanj roared into the gag.

Dale showed Mandy and Tom the sticky side of the tape, most of Sanj's eyebrow hair and eye lashes glued to it in twin, startled arcs.

Smiling, Mandy said, "Now, boys, he did save our baby's life."

His eyes tearing up from the waxing, Sanj nodded his agreement. He was breathing hard against the gag now, sweating in spite of the cool office air.

Tom said to Mandy, "That much is true. It does overlook the fact that he broke into our home and held you and our son at gunpoint, in all likelihood precipitating your labour. It also overlooks the fact that, had he not fainted like a school girl and ended up gift wrapped by a five year old boy and a woman who'd just given birth, he almost certainly would have assassinated everyone in the room." Speaking to Sanj now, Tom said, "But in spite of all that, you do have my sincerest thanks for saving our son."

Sanj gave him an acknowledging nod.

"Now if I remove this gag," Tom said, "will you try to be civil? My wife and child are in the room."

Sanj nodded again.

This time Tom removed the tape, and did so gently. The gag came away with the tape and Tom dropped the whole mess into the garbage can by the desk.

"Thank you," Sanj said. "It tasted like transmission fluid."

"Correct," Mandy said.

Surprising them all, Sanj looked up at Dale and said, "May I have a word with you, Dale?"

* * *

Nervous in spite of the fact that the man was mummy-wrapped to a chair, Dale thought, *What the fuck do you want to talk to me for?* Then he thought he knew and said, "If it's about your brother, I want you to know how sorry I am. I was stoned and afraid and I just…lost it. I still feel sick about it. I'm not a violent person."

Sanj said, "Life is about choices and most of ours were bad. It was really only a matter of time." For a moment Dale thought he was done, but then he said, "But watching my brother die like that—and then being given the opportunity to save a new life… it's been a kind of epiphany for me."

"Sounds pretty Zen there, Sanj," Tom said. "But if you think we're letting you out of that chair before the cops get here, what you're experiencing isn't an epiphany, it's a stroke."

"I am already resigned to my fate," Sanj said. "I am merely trying to shape it into something purposeful."

Tom said, "Let's hear it, then."

"Actually, Tom," Sanj said, "would you mind getting me a glass of water? I'm parched, and all I can taste is that filthy rag."

Dale thought Tom would tell the guy to go fuck a goat, but instead he said, "Sure," and left the room.

In a confiding tone, Sanj started talking again.

* * *

Tom caught himself holding a finger under the tap to make sure the water was cold enough, then he just filled the glass, thinking, *Let him drink it piss warm.*

The gun was digging into his back and he drew it out of his pants and set it on the counter by the sink, checking it to make sure the safety was on.

He paused a moment then and took a deep breath, the

aftermath of the day's events dragging on him like an anchor. His mind was a tilted whirlwind, his thoughts racing and barely coherent, and when he noticed the digital readout on the stove—11:55 p.m.—he could scarcely credit all that had taken place in the last eighteen hours. It felt like days had passed since he'd flown to the outpost cabin, the intervening hours seeming more dreamlike than real. He'd never felt so exhausted, so physically and emotionally drained.

Some birthday.

And with that thought, two things occurred to him simultaneously: one was that all three of the Stokes boys now shared the same birthdate; and the other was something his maternal grandmother used to tell him whenever his life went askew: "It's the outcome that matters."

He was alive. He'd survived a plane crash, a violent encounter with professional assassins, had staged a rescue mission in his own home that had ended in gales of laughter... and he was a dad again, the father of two sweet boys.

Not bad for a day's work.

As curious as he was about what Dale and Sanj were talking about in there, Tom set the glass of water on the counter and opened the fridge, his stomach grinding so hard on him now the room was starting to spin. He hadn't eaten since breakfast and his head was *pounding*.

"Oh, my," he said, peeling back the tinfoil on a baking pan of leftover meatloaf, already sliced into nice thick wafers. He picked one up and took an enormous bite, the stuff delicious even cold.

Then he felt something knuckle-size and hard press against his kidney from behind and heard a woman's husky voice say, "Nice table manners, man," and when he startled the voice said, "Easy, motherfucker, or I'll shoot you where you stand."

Tom felt the muzzle of the gun jabbed hard into his flank, then it was gone and he heard the woman's boot heels clock against the tiles as she took two steps back from him. Sounding amused, she said, "Now turn around and do it slowly."

Still holding a wedge of meatloaf, Tom turned to see a heavily made-up woman of maybe twenty-eight aiming a gun at his head, her index finger hooked firmly around the trigger. Even standing still she appeared to be in motion, vibrating, on the verge of doing something violent, too swift for the eye to see. His glance drifted to the gun he'd left on the counter and the woman said, "Funny. You don't look that stupid."

Abandoning the idea, Tom said, "Who are you?" and the woman said, "Call me Ronnie." She said, "Are you gonna eat that?" and Tom shrugged, only now noticing the speck of white powder on the tip of her nose which, given her wired demeanour, could only be cocaine. She said, "Then give it here," and Tom gave her the chunk of meat, watching with petrified fascination as she gobbled it down like a ravenous chimp. "Mm, shit," she said, specks of meatloaf drizzling to the floor. "Delicious."

Then she was brandishing the gun at him, wanting him to move. "Quietly now, big fella," she said. "Time to have a chat with those fuckweeds in the other room."

* * *

For the past few minutes Dale had been listening to Sanj ramble on about his brother and the dark path they'd chosen, but he had no idea where the guy was headed with it. Was it some sort of ploy to make him feel guilty and maybe cut the crazy fucker loose? If so, it was never gonna work. Truth was, all Dale could think about right now was getting the hell out of here before the cops showed up.

He was about to suggest to Sanj that he get to the point when the man said, "So in light of recent events, I've decided to testify against your brother and Randall Copeland. My cousin Raj does their bookkeeping for them and they've never been anything but rude to him. With Raj's help, I can put them both away for a dozen lifetimes."

"Do that," Dale said, "you won't last a day on the inside."

"Oh, I won't be going to prison," Sanj said. "I'll be going home to India and taking my cousin with me."

"All the people you've killed, you think they'll let you walk?"

"Believe me, if I testify, they'll buy me a first class ticket."

"Well, good luck with that."

"What I'm telling you is, if you keep your head down for a while, you'll be free of them both."

Dale said, "Why would you even care?" the words barely out of his mouth when a gunshot made his ears pop and the chair Sanj was sitting in flipped over backward, blood from the wound in the man's chest speckling Dale's shirt as a familiar voice said, "See if they fly that to India, you piece of shit."

In the background, muted by the whine in Dale's skull, he heard Mandy scream. Then Ronnie's voice again, speaking to him now, Ronnie standing in the doorway behind Tom with his hands raised, Ronnie looking perplexed, peering at him over Tom's shoulder saying, "Now who the fuck are these people and why are you here?"

All Dale could think to say was, "Ronnie. I thought you were dead."

* * *

Moments after the gunshot—Tom had actually *felt* the muzzle blast through his shirt, the woman taking the shot from right next to his waist—Tom heard Steve call out from his room above the office—"Mommy?"—and by instinct tensed to run to him.

Ronnie pressed the gun to his kidney again, freezing him. "Put it out of your mind," she said. "Go sit with the missus. This shouldn't take long."

Tom obeyed. Incredibly, their infant son was still sound asleep. In her usual unflappable way, Mandy whispered, "He's gonna be a good sleeper," and Tom squeezed her warm hand, praying the cops would get here soon and put an end to this mayhem.

Ronnie was still in the doorway with the gun raised, eyes shifting from side to side, saying to Dale now, "Where's the other Paki?"

Dale said, "He's dead."

"How?"

He looked away from her. "I shot him."

Ronnie said, "Dale? Look at me, Dale," and Dale did. She studied him for a moment, sitting there hunched in his chair, as if to assess the likelihood of his claim, then smiled and said, "Well, god damn. Finally grew a pair."

She strode over to him now and kissed him on the mouth. "Miss me?" she said.

Then Steve's voice from upstairs again: "*Mommy.*"

Mandy said, "May I go to him, please?" and Ronnie said, "Nobody's going anywhere." Tom stood and Ronnie swung the gun on him. "Did I say you could move?"

Tom raised his hands and kept going, heading for the desk. Keeping his left hand raised, he used his right to slide open the narrow centre drawer and heard Ronnie cock the pistol. He picked up a bright yellow walkie talkie and showed it to her, easing his way back to the bed now, doing his best to show her he was no threat. He said, "My son has the other one upstairs, okay? I don't want him coming down here."

Ronnie said, "Get it done."

Tom turned on the device and spoke softly into its grille: "Hey, bud, can you hear me, over?"

There was a long pause, then Steve's voice, tinny and alarmed: "Hi, Dad, what was that noise?"

Tom said, "Sorry, pal, that was my fault. I turned the TV on too loud, right in the middle of a gunfight. Did it scare you?"

"Uh huh."

"Well it's nothing to worry about, okay? You go on back to sleep now."

Ronnie said to Tom, "Get it over with," and glanced at Sanj, motionless and bleeding in his overturned chair.

Steve said, "Can you come upstairs?"

"Not right now," Tom said. "Soon, though, okay?"

"Okay, Dad."

Glaring at Ronnie, Tom said, "Goodnight, chum," and turned off the walkie talkie.

Ronnie said, "Toss it on the floor, evil eyes," and Tom complied.

With the gun still aimed at Tom, Ronnie returned her attention to Dale, saying, "Where's the stuff?"

"In the SUV."

"Why the fuck would you leave it out there? Did you lock the doors at least?"

"I can't recall."

"Jesus, Dale, you're like a lost pup." She looked over at the Stokes family, huddled together on the sofa bed. "Now please don't make me ask you again: Who *are* these people and why the fuck are you here?"

"It's a long story."

Ronnie said, "All right. Let's get this over with, then. Go see your friend in Montreal. You can tell me all about it on the road."

Turning her back on Dale, Ronnie started toward the bed, the gun aimed at Mandy now.

Behind her, Dale got to his feet. "Ronnie, what are you doing?"

Ignoring him, Ronnie said to Mandy, "You got a crib or something to put that in?"

Afraid the woman was actually going to shoot his wife, Tom took the baby from her and tried to shield them both with his body. He said, "Look, Ronnie, you don't have to do this. Why don't you just take your stuff and go."

"Sure," Ronnie said, still inching toward them. "And maybe you should snap a few Polaroids before we leave, hand 'em out to the cops as souvenirs. Or better yet, why don't I just jot you a forwarding address?"

"We have nothing to gain by talking to the police," Tom said, sorry now that he'd taken the baby, thinking that if the crazy bitch got just a few feet closer he could rush her, knock her on her ass even if she put a bullet in him. "I just want you gone. You have my word."

Ronnie aimed the gun at the baby and said, "Get the kid out of the way."

* * *

Dale cocked the gun in his hand, aimed it at Ronnie's back and said, "Put it down, Ronnie."

Already smirking, Ronnie did a slow pirouette and aimed her gun at him, her manic green gaze ticking to his trembling gun hand before fixing on his eyes.

"Oh, this is rich," she said. "You're going to shoot *me* now?"

"If I have to."

Ronnie shook her head and laughed, and in what Dale knew was a classic feint started lowering her gun ...

He thought, *Oh, fuck, here it comes,* and closed his eyes.

* * *

On the verge of dropping Dale and saying to fuck with him, Ronnie heard the bitch housewife say, "*Don't*—try it."

Keeping the gun trained on Dale, she shifted her gaze to Mandy, who had a snub-nose semi-auto aimed at her now in a very professional, very confident looking grip. Hubby had gotten to his feet and was moving away from the bed with the baby in his arms.

Mandy said, "I'll be happy to play Wild West with you, 'Ronnie', but before we get to all that, I want you to have a look at those trophies over there."

Ronnie glanced at what looked like a bunch of shooting trophies shelved in a glass case by the wall, then returned her attention to Mandy, a little more warily now.

"They all have my name on them," Mandy said. "So before I turn that greasy forehead of yours into a ten-ring, tell me, how would you like to proceed?"

The coke was seething through her now and Ronnie scowled at Dale, wanting so *badly* to destroy him for his betrayal, but totally unsure of little Miss Mandy over there.

"Please, Ronnie," Dale said, and in spite of herself Ronnie felt a twitch of genuine affection for the guy. "Let's just take the stuff and go. No one has to get hurt."

She stared at him a moment longer, thinking that maybe she'd do just that.

Then she swung the gun on Mandy. "Little *bitch*."

"Ronnie, *no*."

* * *

Mandy squeezed the trigger and saw a neat round hole appear in Ronnie's forehead. Either by intent or reflex, Ronnie got a shot off as she fell, the round ripping through the ceiling above her head.

Steve's room.

Mandy looked at Tom in alarm. Tom handed the baby back to her and left the room running. Still holding his gun, Dale stood staring at Ronnie's body; the finger he'd slid the engagement diamond onto was fluttering.

His sleep broken at last, the baby started crying and Mandy cooed to him, offering her breast, Sanj's backup piece still wafting gunsmoke on the pillow beside her.

* * *

Tom charged into Steve's room to find him sitting on the edge of his bed, clutching his teddy and staring at the bullet hole in the floor. Surrounding it were the remains of the glass hood from his ceiling light.

Tom sat beside him and hugged him tight.

* * *

Tom returned to the office to find Sanj alive and semi-conscious, Dale applying a pressure dressing to the wound in the man's chest. The bloody sheet from the baby's birth had been draped over Ronnie's body and Dale kept glancing at it, a dazed, quizzical expression on his face.

With a nod at Mandy, Tom moved to assist Dale. The baby

was feeding peacefully now, bundled in a blanket in Mandy's arms. She said, "Steve's okay?"

"He's fine," Tom said, helping Dale snug wide strips of adhesive across the already bloody dressing on Sanj's chest. "Poor little guy's so exhausted, he thought he was dreaming. Went straight back to sleep."

Seeing how distraught Dale was, Tom said, "It's okay, man, I've got this." Dale stood, nodding gratefully. Tom said, "You better take off before the police get here."

Dale said, "You mean it?"

Tom smiled. "Just make sure you leave the drugs in the SUV. There's a pickup truck parked in the laneway outside; I spotted it from Steve's room. I'm assuming that's how your girlfriend got here. You should grab the keys and take that."

"What are you going to tell the cops?"

Standing, Tom said, "I'll think of something."

The men shook hands.

Dale found the keys for the pickup in Ronnie's jacket pocket, then shrugged into his coat. "I'm sorry about all this, Mandy," he said.

Mandy smiled and said, "What was it your Granny used to say, Tom?"

"It's the outcome that matters."

Mandy said, "Exactly." She paused a moment to glance at her newborn son, then said, "Can I give you some advice, Dale?"

Dale gave her a nod.

"Find a new line of work."

Smiling, Dale left through the office door.

43

THE PICKUP TRUCK WAS A BRAND NEW Chevy Silverado, and as Dale belted himself in he couldn't help wonder what it must have cost the poor son of a bitch who owned it to allow Ronnie into the cab with him. Probably his life.

Dale could smell her perfume in here, a deeply erotic scent tinged with cigarette smoke that never failed to arouse him. Those first few weeks they'd spent together had been the most intimate and exciting of his life, like being invited into the revved up world of some magnificent supermodel, the kind of woman who, before Ronnie came along, would never even have given him the time of day. She was a wild, fearless creature and he knew he would miss her. Well, certain things about her, anyway.

He backed down the hill to the main road and headed east with no particular destination in mind, the seat radiating a comfortable warmth into his tired ass, Trang's leather brief-case making a nice hand rest on the seat beside him. Leaving the heroin behind—all of it—had been tough, but it was the only thing Tom had asked of him and he owed the man at least that much … and, he realized now, he owed it to himself, as well. He'd gone off the stuff cold turkey numerous times before and knew he was in for a couple of wretched days of withdrawal; but he also knew he could handle it.

He decided then that the first north-south route he came to he'd head south, plug along at the speed limit until he got too sick to drive, then hole up in a motel somewhere and sweat the shit out. After that, who knew?

Someplace warm, he thought, tuning the radio to a classic rock station. *Someplace* hot.

In the oncoming lane two police cars crested a hill and approached him at speed, dome lights strobing. His first instinct was to let up on the accelerator, but he was already doing five klicks under the limit and aborted the urge.

Just hold 'er steady...

The cruisers bore down on him without slowing... and blew past.

Dale breathed.

The tail lights on the trailing car flashed in his rearview for a beat, then went dark. A few seconds later Dale crested the hill. His gaze for the next few minutes kept ticking to the rearview, but there were no cops coming after him. There was no traffic at all.

With a smile playing at the corners of his mouth, Dale turned the radio up and settled in for the long drive ahead, a new artist whose name he didn't catch rockin' out a tune called "Lie Machine." The lyrics made him think of Ronnie.

44

Saturday, January 18, 8:12 a.m.
ONE YEAR LATER

"COME ON, BIG GUY," TOM SAID, playing airplane with a tea-spoon brimmed with pink goo the baby had no intention of allowing into his mouth. The highchair tray already looked like an autopsy slab. "No birthday goo tonight if you don't eat your breakfast goo this morning."

Lightning quick, the little guy shot out a chubby hand and turned the hovering spoon into a catapult, spattering them both with *Beech Nut* Country Breakfast. A dab of it got into Tom's mouth and he nearly gagged. "Okay, bud," he said, "I get it now." He flashed a pleading look at Mandy, but she only smiled and continued stirring her coffee. Steve liked feeding his baby brother, but he was away on a sleepover.

Playing his trump card, Tom said, "Hon, I gotta get air-borne," and the phone rang. With an evil grin, Mandy got up from the table to answer it.

* * *

Dale's Deep Dish Pizza didn't open until ten, but he'd gotten into the habit of coming in early—no big effort since he lived in the apartment above the place—to make sure whoever had closed up the night before had done a good job...but mostly just to savour the reality of it: the custom-made triple-D logo in the window, cool even with the neon switched off; the staff aprons neatly lined up on their hangers in the back, the store logo in full colour on each breast pocket; the heavy pine tables and chairs, the Plexiglass tabletops gleaming under the pot lights; the old Wurlitzer jukebox that had been in the place when he bought it last summer, the thing still working like a charm.

He'd thought of calling Tom numerous times before today, but wanted it to feel just right. And today, on the one year anniversary of their bizarre first meeting, felt just right.

It was Mandy who picked up the phone. He'd hoped for Tom, but this would be just as much fun. He strolled into a beam of tropical sunlight by the big front window and said, "Mrs. Stokes?"

Sounding formal, Mandy said, "That's correct."

"This is Dale at Dale's Deep Dish Pizza calling. Was the pie you ordered for pickup or delivery?"

A pause. "I didn't..."

Grinning, Dale heard the rustle of Mandy covering the mouthpiece, and beyond that, muffled voices. Then Tom was on, saying, "Dale?" and Dale could almost hear the man smiling. He said, "None other," and joined Tom in a good laugh. "Happy birthday, man. You and the boys."

"Thanks, buddy," Tom said. "Little early for pizza, don't you think?"

"Not for Dale's Deep Dish it ain't."

"You used the name?"

"Indeed I did. Figured it was only fair, since you christened your new son 'Dale.'"

Tom chuckled. "Try Joseph Michael," he said. "I thought of it, though, I really did. Almost said it out loud to Mandy once, but decided not to risk a divorce."

The men laughed again and Tom said, "Where are you, man?"

"Turns out Arubians love deep dish pizza. And they're not all that big on extradition treaties, so it's been a perfect fit."

"Aruba," Tom said. "You son of a gun, you did it. Good for you, man." He said, "I was sorry to hear about your brother. Well, not really, but you know what I mean."

"I do. And thanks. I mean, the prick did try to have me killed. But he was my brother. Moral of the story, when Randall Copeland says twenty-four hours, he *means* twenty-four hours."

"Well, ol' Randy'll be away for at least that many years. Did you follow the trial?"

"Sure did," Dale said. "Sanj kept his word."

"Speaking of Sanj, I got a postcard from the man a few months back. Says he started an EMT course in Bangladesh last fall."

Dale said, "Well, I'll be god damned…"

ABOUT THE AUTHOR

Sean Costello has been practicing anaesthesiology in Sudbury since 1981. Previous novels include *Eden's Eyes*, 1989; *The Cartoonist*, 1990; *Captain Quad*, 1991, all published by Pocket Books (*Captain Quad* was reprinted by Scrivener Press, 2011); *Sandman*, 2000; *Finders Keepers*, 2002; and *Here After*, Scrivener Press, 2008. *Here After* and *Squall* have been optioned for films. *Here After* was short-listed for the Northern 'Lit' Award (Ontario Library Services—North), and received Honorable mention for the Sunburst Award.